BIRDSPELL

MORE STORIES FOR TEENS AND TWEENS
BY VALERIE SHERRARD

*If you enjoy humor, these books are
very good choices for you.

BIRDSPELL

VALERIE SHERRARD

Canada Council
for the Arts
Conseil des Arts
du Canada

 ONTARIO ARTS COUNCIL
CONSEIL DES ARTS DE L'ONTARIO
an Ontario government agency
un organisme du gouvernement de l'Ontario

 ONTARIO
CREATES
ONTARIO
CRÉATIF

Canadian
Heritage
Patrimoine
canadien

Canadä

The publisher gratefully acknowledges the support of the Canada Council
for the Arts and the Ontario Arts Council for its publishing program.
We acknowledge the financial support of the Government of Canada through
the Canada Book Fund (CBF) for our publishing activities, and the Government of
Ontario through Ontario Creates, an agency of the Ontario Ministry of Culture,
and the Ontario Book Publishing Tax Credit Program.

LIBRARY AND ARCHIVES CANADA CATALOGUING IN PUBLICATION

Title: Birdspell / Valerie Sherrard.
Names: Sherrard, Valerie, author.
Identifiers: Canadiana (print) 20200340786 | Canadiana (ebook) 20200340816 |
ISBN 9781770866133 (softcover) | ISBN 9781770866140 (HTML)
Classification: LCC PS8587.H3867 B57 2021 | DDC jc813/.54—dc23

United States Library of Congress Control Number: 2020950458

Cover art: David Jardine
Interior text design: Tannice Goddard, tannicegdesigns.ca

Printed and bound in Canada.
Manufactured by Friesens in Altona, Manitoba in February 2021.

DCB Young Readers
AN IMPRINT OF CORMORANT BOOKS INC.
260 SPADINA AVENUE, SUITE 502, TORONTO, ONTARIO, M5T 2E4
www.dcbyoungreaders.com
www.cormorantbooks.com

In memory of John Ryan Turner
If only we had known

BIRDSPELL

One

When you're walking home from school beside a girl who's promised to give you something you really, really want, getting slugged is about the farthest thing from your mind. Which is why I was unprepared for the palm-slam that knocked me sideways into a recycle bin. It went down without a fight, and took me with it.

"Hey!" That one-word protest *should* have been me, but strangely enough it was *her*. My assailant. Izelle of the lightning-quick, came-out-of-nowhere strike.

I scrambled to my feet, resisting the urge to dust myself off. Enough dignity had already been sacrificed to the blue bin.

"You're joking, right?" she said. "About not having a cell phone?"

That's the problem if you live in Normal. You think the whole world should sync itself to your way of life.

"Nope," I said. "I really don't have one." And then, in a stroke of genius I added, "We're what you call minimalists."

This was not strictly true. But it might let me explain a bizarre part of my life to her, which was something I knew I'd be doing in a matter of minutes.

"Is that like some kind of religion?" she asked.

I listen carefully. So, I'd heard the *way* she said "religion" and it was casual and curious. No hidden sneer. Safe.

"Yep," I said, but I knew immediately I'd made a mistake. If she googled it, she'd know I was lying.

"That is," I backtracked, "it's not *exactly* a religion, but some people kind of look at it like it is."

Izelle stopped walking. Her fists found her hips and her mouth went into a pout that I could easily picture her practicing in front of a mirror.

"Tell me the *truth*, Corbin — are you some kind of weirdo?"

"Of course not." That's true. I'm reasonably average. Her question made me wonder, though, how innocently trusting she was to ask something like that. Would a weirdo admit it? Or even know that's what they were?

At the same time, I wished I knew her well enough to calm any misgivings she was having. But our contact has been limited to a few weeks and a couple of short conversations.

Izelle is in the class I joined less than a month ago. Grade six at Middling Academy. So far it's not the worst school I've ever had to switch to mid-year. I gave them points right off for not assigning me a buddy like the last place did. At that school the guy they put in charge of helping me settle in had loads of free time to devote to the task since he was essentially friendless. Maybe they were trying to kill two birds with one stone. I don't know, but it didn't end well.

That was behind me now, while in front of me was this girl. A girl I know nothing about.

No, that's not true. I know one thing. Izelle is a chatterer, which is not a trait that hides in a corner and one day jumps out to surprise you. The first conversation we had was kick-started when I asked her where the school computer lab was. She rewarded me with a prattle of information that included stuff about library programs and social groups, and she only paused when she was desperate for air. I almost missed the actual answer — the lab was in a room off the library — in the flood of words.

She's nice enough though, I guess. That's more or less "whatever" to me. What matters is that she's giving me her parakeet. At least, I *hope* she's giving it to me.

Before that can happen, she insists on checking out my apartment. The thought of taking anyone there almost made me back out, but I really want that bird.

Not that I've been hankering for a bird specifically. I'd take almost any kind of pet, really, as long as it was some kind of company.

It was last week when I overheard Izelle telling her friend Mandy she had to find a new home for her parakeet. I asked her about it later that day, but she said Mandy had dibs on it and she'd let me know if that didn't work out.

"Sure, okay," I told her, adding as if it was an afterthought, "I didn't catch the price. How much is it?"

"It's free. Bird, cage, cover, toys — *everything*. My mother says selling a family pet is bad luck."

Then there was a long and convoluted explanation about why the bird had to be re-homed. Something about allergies — I didn't actually catch who was allergic before she went on to say her great-aunt had just moved in and her father had switched to a home office, although how, or even *if*, the aunt and dad parts had anything to do with why the bird had to go I couldn't say. Since someone else was already planning to take it, I wasn't exactly motivated to pay attention.

I did catch the bird's name, which is Sitta.

"You probably think that's a weird name, right?" Izelle asked. "But it's *meaningful* when you know the story behind it."

I raised my eyebrows, which she mistakenly took to mean "how interesting, please go on." Whether she needed the encouragement or not — I doubt this very much — Izelle did indeed go on.

"It's short for the actual, proper name for the Rose-Ringed Parakeet, which is *Psittacula Krameri.*"

"Huh," I said.

"You can't tell from the way it sounds, because the P is silent, but it's spelled P-S-I-T-T-A-C-U-L-A K-R-A-M-E-R-I."

"Ah," I said.

"So, if you drop the P, which is silent anyway, and look at the next five letters, there you have it! Sitta. Cool huh?"

"Mmm," I said.

Like I said, I've wanted a pet for years. A dog would have been my first choice, but I like cats too. Neither had ever been an option. I could have had a fish any-time, but that didn't interest me. A bird, on the other hand, should be pretty good company, especially when the place gets too quiet. A free bird — now *that* was perfect. I can usually find a way to scrounge together a few bucks when I need to, but if they'd been charging for the bird and cage and other supplies, it would have been out of reach.

And of course since someone else "had dibs" it was still out of reach until the end of class today when Izelle hurried up to me.

"Hey, Corbin! Mandy's mother is being unreasonable and won't let her have Sitta. Do you still want him?"

"Sure!" My head started to race with plans. Izelle broke into them almost immediately.

"I just need to see your place first. You know, to be sure Sitta will approve of it. I might as well go home with you now."

My brain froze, which explains why my mouth said, "Uh, okay."

So there we were, on the way to the place I call home. We'd resumed walking as soon as I'd assured her I was not, in fact, a weirdo. A denial was apparently all the proof she required.

And then we were there, climbing the stairs to the second floor, making our way to the last unit on the right.

I'd more or less decided it didn't really matter if I got Sitta, because my chances were about to go way, way down.

And of course, as soon as the door was open and she'd taken a few steps into the apartment, out it came. The question I'd been expecting.

"Um, Corbin? Where's your furniture?"

Two

The short answer was: nowhere. Aside from a couple of mattresses, two cushions, and a folding stool that makes sure Mom's cherished aloe plant gets some sun, we *have* no furniture. Anyone I brought to the apartment was guaranteed to ask about that. One of the top ten reasons I never invite anyone over.

"Oh, furniture," I said offhandedly. "Yeah, we don't have any."

"You have *no furniture*?"

"Remember? I told you we're minimalists?"

"But you have *nothing*. That's not minimal — it's zero!"

I knew by the way she eased back a couple of steps that the nearly-empty apartment was unnerving her.

"Okay, so it's kind of a strange story," I said slowly, buying time to think. "And this isn't something I would tell to just anybody because most people wouldn't get it. But I think you might."

Her face relaxed a little.

And then behind us, I heard a door open.

It wasn't the door to my apartment — I hadn't closed that yet — so it could only be Mr. Zinbendal, our elderly neighbor across the hall.

Izelle whirled around and offered him a shy little wave.

Mr. Zinbendal was in his usual attire — faded brown pants that sagged in the knees and bum, a pale checked shirt, and a dark gray cardigan that was so loose it could have wrapped around him twice.

He didn't wave back to Izelle. What he *did* offer was a heavy sigh and a wrinkled scowl. His usual greeting.

Then he shoved his door shut. Ka-lack!!

I could see Sitta sliding out of reach. Who'd want to see their pet go to a home with no furniture and someone that crabby across the hall? Except, when Izelle spoke, her voice was soft and sad.

"The poor man."

"What, *him*?" I could hardly believe the biggest sour-puss of a neighbor we've ever had — and we've lived in a *lot* of places — was being described so sympathetically. In the few short weeks we've been here, Zinbendal's long face has already gotten under Mom's skin more than once.

"Yes, of course," Izelle said. "He looks so terribly unhappy."

"Yeah well —" I shrugged and shut up. Some thoughts are better left unfinished.

"You were going to tell me why you have no furniture," Izelle reminded me.

"Sure," I said. I closed the door so there'd be no further interruptions from Mr. Zinbendal and ushered her into the living room area. "These cushions are really comfortable — go ahead and try one."

Izelle positioned herself doubtfully over the larger of the two — an ugly orange and green pillow I scored for a quarter at a yard sale last summer. It had been marked two bucks but it hadn't sold by late morning. That's the best time to get bargains, because no one wants to lug a bunch of unsold stuff back inside.

It's not easy the first time you try to lower yourself onto a cushion when there's nothing to hold onto. I tried to help by demonstrating a deep squat and a gentle backward flop, but ended up banging my head on the wall. That happens regularly.

"Are you okay?" Izelle asked. She knelt on the floor and easily maneuvered herself onto her cushion. Without a head injury.

"Fine," I said. "So, anyway, about the decor. I need you to promise you won't tell this to anyone else."

"I promise," she said solemnly.

"You've heard about people who were raised by wolves, right?" I said.

Izelle blinked slowly. "I think those are just stories," she said.

"Oh, no. It's rare, but it really happens."

Izelle said nothing.

"See, my mother grew up in circumstances a bit like that. Years ago, there was a terrible family tragedy — she still can't talk about it — and the only survivors were Mom and her grandmother. Because her grandma was old and blind, the children's agency wanted to take my mom away from her. To keep that from happening, her grandma took her to live in the wild. They only survived because some of the animals in the area helped them. My mom lived there, far from civilization, up until the old woman died and was buried deep in the forest. But even after she made her way back to the city, Mom could never get used to all the trappings of everyday life. Like furniture."

Izelle's eyes had grown rounder and rounder as I spoke. "Wow!" she said.

I nodded gravely.

Then she laughed.

"Okay, so what's the real reason?" she said.

"Ha ha," I said. "Thought I had you there for a minute.

Okay, so the truth is we really *are* minimalists, only kind of in the extreme. My mom is an environmental fanatic. She's always going on about reducing our carbon footprint and stuff like that. *That's* the truth about why we live this way."

Three

Yeah, okay, so that second story was also a lie.

I wasn't about to tell Izelle how Mom gave up on furniture two years and three moves ago. That was when we moved from Green Lake Boulevard to Charles Street.

We'd spent an hour or so lugging our personal and household stuff, most of which had been tossed into boxes. They were in pretty bad shape, our boxes. Sides beaten down, bent, and gouged from previous moves.

Once everything had been shoved into the beat-up old van Mom had back then, I was anxious to get out of there. When you've been encouraged to leave a place and you're reasonably sure the other tenants know it, standing around on the sidewalk doesn't fill you with pride.

"Where's Mike anyway?" I asked.

Mike has been around, off and on, for as long as I can remember. Besides my mom, he's been the one fairly constant person in my life, no matter what part of the city we've been living in at any given time.

Mike shows up for supper now and then, and sometimes hangs around for the evening. He and Mom have known each other pretty much all their lives because they grew up just a few houses apart, but that isn't why they're friends.

Originally, Mike was best friends with Mom's older brother George, an uncle I never met. George died in a bizarre factory accident when he was only twenty-seven and I think Mike is honoring their friendship by watching out for his buddy's kid sister. That's just a guess; I've never asked him.

Compared to some of the other friends Mom has had over the years, Mike is pretty close to normal. Except maybe when he's showing off some of the wooden figures he whittles. The last ones were supposed to be chess pieces, but I could barely tell them apart.

Anyway, on that particular day, Mike was supposed to bring his truck to help us move the furniture.

"He can't make it," Mom said.

The way she said it, kind of defensive, told me they'd had an argument. That happens often enough and they always patch up the friendship, eventually. None of which was helpful at that moment.

"Then how are we going to move the rest of our stuff?" I asked.

"You know what, Corbin, I've been thinking. We've been prisoners without even realizing it, dragging all that stuff around from place to place. And what did it ever do for us?"

What did our furniture ever do for us? Now that was an opening for backtalk if ever there was one, but it wasn't the time for sass. I said nothing.

"You want open concept? I'll *give* you open concept," Mom added. She tucked her red-at-the-time hair behind her ears and squared her shoulders.

"I don't want open concept," I muttered, not too loud, but apparently loud enough.

"I guess you like being a prisoner to *things*, then, do you?"

Mom's hands fluttered into the air, a sure sign she was winding up.

"Sorry," I said quickly. I went around the van, got into the passenger seat, and shut the door. I stared straight ahead, even when Mom climbed in and pulled her door closed — harder than she needed to.

"I'll have you know that I have more than enough to deal with without you adding to my problems, Corbin."

Her problems.

"Can we just go?" I said, still not looking at her even though I felt her eyes on me.

I knew she was dropping it when I heard the sigh. Mom has a way of sighing that's long and deep and full of disappointment with just about everything in her life, including me. Maybe especially me. I didn't care. I just wanted out of there. She didn't speak to me until a couple of days later. A victory, even that small, has its price.

Charles Street, where we moved to that day, was one of the better places we've lived, even without the furniture. The emptiness of an unfurnished apartment was strange, but I got used to it eventually and when we had to leave there it made moving a whole lot easier.

Most recently, we landed here, in a second-floor apartment on Westlester Street. And there I was, sitting next to Izelle, trying to put a reasonable-sounding spin on why the place looked like it was inhabited by squatters.

She'd stopped staring at me and had moved her attention to the open spaces around us, trailing her eyes across barren floors and walls. When she stood up, staring me down with the set jaw of someone who's made a decision, I was already saying goodbye to the bird.

"This is *not* what I was expecting," she said.

Of course it wasn't. I got to my feet so I could face her without feeling like a toddler.

"It's absolutely *perfect*," Izelle said, lifting her hands and letting them drift apart like she was conducting an invisible choir.

I turned into a stone. No reaction whatsoever. Because I wasn't sure what was coming next. She could be sincere, or she could be checking to see how gullible I was.

"Sitta will *love* all this open space!" she said. It sounded like she meant it.

The next thing I knew, she was right in my face. Her nose almost touched mine and for a second, I had the alarming thought that she was going to kiss me.

"You'll let him out to fly around sometimes, right?"

"Uh —"

"Mom never did. She always worried he'd you-know-what on the furniture, but you *have* none."

And just like that, I became an approved bird owner. It was an exciting few seconds, until she mentioned there were rules attached, which she called the Conditions of Adoption. As if they'd been drafted by a lawyer or something.

As she recited them, Izelle counted these conditions off on her fingers.

1.) Something I didn't actually catch, although I think it was about Sitta's diet

2.) A stern warning to NEVER EVER NO MATTER WHAT, EVER, EVER let him out of the cage if there was a window or door open

3.) Visitation rights for Izelle, at least once a week

The list didn't end there, but that's where I stopped hearing her. Was she kidding? She expected me to let her come over to see Sitta every week?

It was pure luck that it had been safe to bring her here today. But a regular arrangement? That would be way too risky. As unfortunate as it was, I knew the second she mentioned visitation, there was no way I could take the bird. Out of politeness, I let her finish talking. (I believe she wrapped up at number eight.) Then it was time to give her the bad news.

Except, for the second time that day, something overrode my brain.

"Sure," I said. "No problem."

Four

Sitta moved in two days later. Izelle's father, Mr. Renda, delivered her, along with the bird, cage, and various supplies, including enough toys to make a small child jealous. These were contained in a collapsible clothes hamper.

I'd been waiting at the front entry, ready with half a dozen excuses to keep Mr. Renda from seeing our naked abode. But when he jumped out of the car and started to unload Sitta's belongings onto the sidewalk, he said he had to make a quick phone call and then he'd give us a hand.

"Great," I said. Then I sped up the stairs with the first load and made it back to the car for the rest before he finished his call.

He made an apologetic face as I began gathering up the remaining supplies. I gave him a "no problem" wave and he offered a half smile as Izelle and I started back toward the building.

She carried the cage, which was covered, and a bag of leafy produce. I balanced a couple of heavy boxes that I later discovered were full of newspapers for lining the cage. Once everything was upstairs I finally got to meet my bird.

My first thought was, *Wow, is he ever green*. It was like someone had made a bird from electric algae, and added a blood-red beak and orange circles to accent the tiny black beads of his eyes. There was bright yellow under his tail feathers and a darkly underlined pink ring around his neck. That made sense for a bird commonly known as a Rose-Ringed Parakeet.

He was spectacular.

I have to admit, Sitta seemed a whole lot less impressed with me than I was with him. He cast a haughty look my way and went back to preening. I found his attitude amusing, and besides, I was willing to give him time.

Izelle insisted that she should be the one to show him around, which she did. It was kind of cute, although a bit sad. Then she apologized that she couldn't stay to settle him in.

"Dad's waiting for me, so —"

She broke off in mid-sentence and bit down on her lower lip. Tears were starting to fill her eyes.

"I should give you some privacy," I said quickly. "So you can say goodbye and whatever."

I stepped into my room, regretting immediately that I hadn't chosen the bathroom. Not that I needed to go, but there's a loud fan in there that would have drowned out some of the sobs and bits of conversation I'd rather not have heard.

Finally, there was a patch of silence, followed by footsteps that stopped at my bedroom door. Izelle's sad voice floated in.

"I'm going now, Corbin. See you tomorrow."

"Okay," I said. That sounded too cheerful so I added, "Don't forget you'll see Sitta every week."

If she answered, I didn't hear it. A moment later the apartment door clunked shut and I went out and escorted Sitta and his belongings into my room.

Mom arrived home about an hour later, just as I was getting out the bowls for our supper — KD with chopped tomato. Her favorite comfort food, which I hoped would put her in a good frame of mind when I broke the news that we'd acquired a pet bird.

I passed her a bowl of food before hoisting myself up on the counter and digging into my own.

"How was work?" I said.

"Same old, same old."

I turned a few phrases in my head. After a moment I settled on, "Something interesting happened at school today."

"Yeah?"

"A girl in my class was giving away her pet parakeet. And no one else wanted it so we got it!"

Mom stopped chewing. She gave me a look that I can only describe as a dead-eye stare. I sat my bowl down and slid off the counter, just in case.

"I don't know what's wrong with you, Corbin, seriously I don't," she said at last. "Why would we want a bird no one else would take?"

"He's a really nice bird," I insisted. "His name is Sitta. You want to see him?"

"You mean this creature is here *now*?" She glanced around. "Where is it?"

"In my bedroom."

"Well, that's where it can stay."

Not a great outcome, but I was good with that until about an hour later when Mom barged into my room with an envelope labeled, "Eviction Notice." (For the bird. The law says she has to feed and house *me* until I'm sixteen.) She gave me a pointed look and taped it to the cage.

Mom apparently hadn't registered Sitta's name, since the paper inside the envelope simply said: *Bird, You have thirty days to get out of my apartment.*

Most parents, on finding an unwanted bird in their house, would insist on its immediate removal. Not Mom. She's pretty much an expert on tenants' rights and luckily, she was applying some of those to Sitta.

That gave me time to figure out my next move if Mom didn't change her mind in the meantime — something that was not only possible, but likely. Mom is kind of the queen of about-faces. One thing still worried me, though. I took the note to her.

"There's no date on this," I pointed out. I knew I needed the thirty days locked in solid.

"Let me see that!" She grabbed it from my hand and looked it over. "Well, it's from today, obviously."

"Yeah, but what if, uh, Sitta forgets when he got it?"

"The bird can't read, Corbin." Mom shook her head heavily and looked at me with sorrowful eyes. "Honestly, I don't know who's going to think for you when you're grown."

I passed her a pen. "Right. So maybe you should add the date in case I get mixed up."

"Where's the calendar?"

"Today is January twenty-sixth."

She wrote that at the top of Sitta's eviction notice. "Okay, so the bird has until February —"

She paused, counting off the days on her fingers. "February twenty-fifth. And then it's *out*. Got it?"

"Got it." I folded Sitta's eviction notice and stuck it in my jeans.

"Don't worry," I told him later. "Mom changes her mind a lot. She's just in a bad mood right now."

I didn't tell him not to bet his birdseed on what Mom might do next.

Five

Three weeks before I was born my mother was diagnosed with bipolar disorder. She was twenty-three at the time and had been living on her own for a couple of years, basically since her parents moved to a little town on the east coast. One Thursday evening, sporting an enormous baby bump, she tottered into a busy intersection and started directing traffic.

I heard about this from my father during one of his brief visits, which happen once or twice a year at the most. He admitted he was horrified when it happened, but by the time he was describing the scene to me years later, it had become hilarious in memory. My very pregnant mother, waddling around, waving her arms and shouting, first at motorists and then at the police.

Apparently, she was convinced she'd come up with a superior way to guide traffic and when she couldn't get anyone to listen to her idea, she thought a demonstration would do the trick.

Her doctor signed her into a psych ward, where she stayed until a couple of days before my arrival. The first, but not the last time she's been hospitalized for her illness.

Don't get me wrong. It's not common for Mom to do things as bizarre as the traffic fiasco. She's just kind of all over the place sometimes. If there's one thing I've learned to expect from her, it's change. Her most determined plans can be overturned, sometimes within hours or even minutes.

So, I wasn't seriously worried she'd follow through on her threat to evict Sitta. The bigger problem of the moment was getting him food. I'd done some research at school and discovered this wasn't going to be a simple matter of picking up a bag of birdseed now and then. Sitta needed a lot more than that. About eighty percent of his diet had to be sprouts and vegetables, with a bit of fruit now and then. And that wasn't even the end of it. There were herbs and eggs and other things.

Izelle had brought along a couple of big bags of food for him. One was loaded with different kinds of seeds and pellets and the other one was stuffed with a mixture of green leafy stuff. I didn't even know what half of it was, but figured there was enough of it to buy me time to get a plan in place. As in, a way to make some cash.

I've learned over the years that there are always people willing to pay for odd jobs, even in a barely-middle-class building like this. So I grabbed a sheet of paper and wrote, "Help with errands or chores. Corbin Hayes, Unit 2H." I added a border with highlighter to make it more noticeable and took it down to the laundry room.

All laundry rooms smell the same. I like them best when they're warm and the air is moist and soapy, which was the case when I stepped inside and looked around for a bulletin board. I had tape in my back pocket just in case, but it wasn't needed. An old cork board was on the wall over the line of four washers, two of which were running.

A girl with a bright green lip spike was leaning back against one of them holding a cell phone about three inches from her face. Next to her, and blocking my access to the board, was a stroller with a little girl, judging by the outfit. She looked at me immediately. The girl with the phone very deliberately did *not*.

"Excuse me," I said.

She did something squinty with one eye, like a bit of lint had just gotten into it, while raising the eyebrow over the other. It was an impressively bored gesture.

"Do you mind if I move your baby for a sec?" I said. "I just need to reach this board."

"*My* baby? What are you, insane? I'm *fifteen*," she said.

She leaned forward, grabbed the handle of the stroller, and gave it a slight push. It was just enough to send it banging into a table in the center of the room. The child started to cry.

"Nice," the girl said, like I was the one who'd shoved the stroller.

I stretched across the washer and stuck my ad up with a yellow pushpin while the girl sighed loudly, stuffed her phone into a pocket and crossed over to the howling child.

"What did that BAD boy do?" she said, while she scooped the kid up and hugged her. The crying stopped as abruptly as it had started.

"BAD!" said the toddler.

"Hey, I didn't do anything," I said.

"BAD!" she repeated. She looked to the older girl for confirmation and received an approving nod.

"That's right, pea pod," she said.

I noticed her look changed while she was holding the kid. The hostility was still there, but it had dropped to about four out of ten, where it had been a solid eight before.

"Well, then," I said, addressing pea pod. "I'm awful sorry and I promise to never do such a dastardly deed again."

There might have been a twitch at the corner of the mean girl's mouth, I'm not sure. She shifted the kid to her other hip, ignoring me, and said, "*Maybe* we'll think about forgiving the BAD boy, huh?"

"BAD!" said pea pod happily.

My cue to leave.

Six

"What do you think you're doing? What the *H-E-double hockey sticks* is this?"

Mom doesn't believe in cussing. Ever. Even in the throes of a spit-flying, insanely angry rant, she'll never go beyond her own brand of expletives. Some of them would be enough to make me laugh if I didn't know better.

I'd barely stepped through the door into our apartment when this particular question came flying at me. It sent me into rapid-process mode, where my brain started lining up the facts.

1.) School just got out, which means Mom *should* still be at work.

2.) She's holding a piece of paper, which is obviously the source of her anger at the moment, so I need to get closer to it.

"You don't need to think for one second that you can pull this kind of stunt in my house and get away with it," Mom said. Her eyes darted at me, dark and full of challenge.

3.) The paper in her hand looks familiar, but I'm not sure …wait, is it …

"Whatever you're up to — and I'm not sure I even want to know, Corbin — I can tell you right now, it's going to stop. Stop in its flipping flapping tracks. So don't expect to smooth talk your way out of this one."

4.) Yes it is! She's holding the ad I stuck up in the laundry room a few days ago. Which makes me wonder how long she's been home and *what she's been up to.*

"I'm just going to check on Sitta," I said. And I moved fast, but not so fast that I was going to set off her chase response. Except, I miscalculated.

The paper dropped from her hands and she was in motion, heading toward me. I broke into a run, skidded around the corner into my room, and almost had the door pushed shut when she crashed into it, sending me flying and almost falling herself. Thankfully, she grabbed the doorknob and regained her footing.

"Do *not* walk away from me when I'm talking to you," she warned, using her sepulcher voice. The one that makes the skin on my neck crawl.

"Mom —"

"Don't you 'Mom' me you little sneak. Slinking around, cooking up your schemes, thinking you can get ahead of me." She laughed, and the sound was more chilling than the voice.

Sitta's cage looked undisturbed. The cover didn't appear to have been moved since I'd put it in place before school.

"*Look at me* when I'm talking to you!"

"Sorry." I edged closer to the cage and tugged the cover off. Sitta looked around, turning his head side to side. The twist in my gut loosened. And what had I been thinking anyway? Mom wouldn't hurt an innocent bird. I get scared about nothing sometimes.

This particular innocent bird knows that when the cover comes off his cage, food is on its way. He doesn't wait patiently if it isn't.

"I'll be back with some grub in a minute buddy," I told him.

Sitta had no interest in hearing promises. He wanted

food that very second and when it didn't come he let me know he was displeased. The demanding screeches he sent up weren't exactly calming to Mom's mood.

"Where do you think we're going to get the time or resources to screen all those people?" Mom demanded as I edged past her. "It's not like I have the right connections. Not anymore."

"You're right. I wasn't thinking," I said.

She followed as I turned left into the kitchen and tugged open the cupboard where the bag of birdseed was. I grabbed it and some green leaves from the fridge and started back to my room.

"Stop that!" Mom said. "How am I supposed to get to the bottom of this with you running around all over the place?"

My laundry room ad was still where she'd dropped it. I let the bag of feed slip to the floor and scooped up the paper as I retrieved it.

"I'm just going to feed Sitta," I said. "Could you pick out something for supper while I'm doing that? And then I'll be able to totally focus on what you're telling me."

She hesitated, then agreed and began to look through the cupboards while I hurried to my room, shoved food into the cage, told Sitta I'd be back soon to let him out, and dashed back to the kitchen.

I'd been gone two minutes at the most, but Mom had already assembled a can of beans, an egg, ketchup, three cheese slices, a box of frozen waffles, and a blueberry bagel on the counter. As I looked them over she added two packages of ramen noodles, a nearly empty jar of sweet and sour sauce, and a whisk.

"Not bad, huh?" she said, waving her hand over it like a game show model.

"Great selection," I said. I could tell she'd already moved away from the imaginary problems my ad was going to cause. "How about you relax for a bit while I fix our supper?"

"I have no time to relax," she snapped. "There are things to be done."

"You're not tired from work?" I asked casually. I already knew what the answer was going to be, but I no longer try to avoid hearing it. I did that a lot when I was younger — tried to keep the subject on anything else as long as I could, clutching a thread of hope that it wasn't happening again.

"Nope!" she said. "I quit my job!"

There it was. As usual, she made it sound like a huge, exciting announcement. Wonderful. Thrilling.

I put the waffles, cheese slices, and egg back into the

fridge. Beans on toast was about all I thought I could handle right then.

"Well?" Mom's hands floated up and out, palms toward me. "Aren't you going to ask me why?"

"Sure. Why?"

"Be*cause* —"

Big dramatic pause. I knew I was expected to look over, which I did, while tapping the beans into a small pot.

"I'm going out on my own!"

"Wow, Mom! Doing what?" I stuck two slices of bread into the toaster and shoved it down. As I did that, it struck me that it was way too early for supper. Mom being home had thrown me off. I popped the bread up and out, stuck it back into the bag, and turned off the burner the pot of beans was sitting on.

Mom had been talking the whole time. I tried to focus.

"… which is why there's such a shortage of people who want to work. Now, with my agency, people will be guaranteed a living wage and all the benefits. You can't have people going outside the country for some of these things. I can't fix that, at least not right away, but it could be a focus of the second stage, once the parent company is established and hits the top one hundred list."

Clearly, I'd missed the first part of her plan — not that it mattered.

What did matter was that Mom's paychecks would stop coming and I'd have to somehow persuade her to apply for assistance and try to make sure the rent got paid and food got bought until this crisis had passed. And I knew there was almost no chance I could talk her into doing any of that.

Sitta wasn't the only one I was going to have to worry about feeding.

Seven

"I was thinking I'd come visit Sitta after school today."

Izelle's face was pink and bright. Moisture circled her eyes, making it obvious she'd been crying. Of course I knew why. She missed the bird. And why wouldn't she? He's more excellent than I could ever have imagined. Whenever he and I have the place to ourselves he's about the best company a bird could be, hopping around on my shoulder, leaning over and looking right in my face, talking in bird-speak, and just generally being entertaining. Plus he's a great listener.

It hadn't even been a full week since he'd moved in with me, but I wasn't surprised she was anxious to see him. The problem at that moment was, I couldn't let her. I wanted to, but I couldn't. With Mom not working, she was in and out, trailing wild energy and scattered thoughts behind her. There was no way could I risk Izelle meeting my mother, not while she was blasting around in overdrive.

"Uh, yeah. I really wish you could," I told her, meaning it. "But my mom's home sick this week and I can't take anyone there until she's better."

"What is it, like, a cold?"

"No, it's quite a bit more serious than that," I said, in case next week was a problem too. It's hard to predict how long Mom's manic stages are going to last.

"Oh." Izelle's expression was instantly solemn. Caring, even. "I'm really sorry. Is she going to be okay?"

"We hope so," I said in a sad, ominous tone. Izelle blinked a couple of times before reaching out to give my hand an awkward pat. Then she turned and disappeared down the hall.

I knew if I had to, I could probably build on this lie and drag it out until she gave up on seeing Sitta. Or we moved. That could solve a lot of future problems. But it seemed a pretty low thing to do and I made up my mind to leave it as a last resort.

The apartment was empty when I got home and for a minute I wished I'd taken a chance and brought Izelle along. That thought disappeared less than five minutes after I'd fed Sitta, which is when the door flew open and Mom sped in carrying a large shopping bag.

My heart sank.

"Corbin, quick love, come help your mother!" she called.

I was already moving toward her, wanting to know what she'd wasted whatever small amount of money we had on, and hoping to find the receipt so I could sneak anything returnable back for a refund as soon as I had a chance.

"I'm on the verge of something *so* big," Mom said as I lifted the bag from her arms and looked inside. "Son, we are going to be rich!"

"I'll put this in the closet for now," I said. "So nothing gets bent or wrecked." At first glance, I'd seen presentation folders, name tags, pens, and various other office-type supplies. It was easy to picture it falling victim to a frenzy of enthusiasm — shuffled and spread across the floor, stepped on, crumpled, torn, and marked up. In other words: non-returnable.

Mom didn't argue, mainly because she was busy telling me about all the money we were going to have. We were going to be rolling around in piles of cash morning, noon, and night. Not the safest way to store our imaginary future fortune.

"Won't that attract burglars?" I said.

"No silly, because we'll be living in a gated community

and have all kinds of security for our mansion!"

Mom laughed, head back, mouth round and turned upward as though she was letting sound bubbles rise and escape. It was infectious and I couldn't keep from smiling at her delight.

She grabbed my hand then and whirled me around, her eyes snapping with joy and excitement. Even with a familiar feeling of dread snaking its way through me, I found myself laughing and joining in with Mom's enthusiasm.

Before I knew it we were galloping around and around, naming all the things we planned to buy and singing snatches of "If I Had a Million Dollars."

"You know what?" Mom said, stopping abruptly. "We should celebrate!"

"Pancakes!" I said quickly. "Yes!"

"I was kind of thinking we'd eat out," Mom said.

"Letter pancakes!" I said. "We can do some with our initials and some with dollar signs. They can be green."

She was wavering, but not quite sold.

"*Please*?"

"Oh, all right. I want to tell you the whole plan anyway and we can't risk someone overhearing it."

And she did. She told me about it while we made

the pancakes and while we ate. She was still going on afterward, while I hunched silently on my cushion in the corner of the living room. The details morphed as she talked, swelling and stretching into new shapes. Her words tumbled and rolled. The landscape of Mom's plan, as always, was shifting, rushing into mountainous slopes before swooping down, leveling, and rising up again.

The plan itself was actually simple.

"I will have the *only* employment agency that insists on its clients being paid a wage well above the minimum amount imposed by law!" she proclaimed. "It's brilliant. Brilliant! Clients will flock to me in droves because no one else will be getting them a decent income. And that's just the start — the tip of the iceberg. There will be branches everywhere before long, with vast franchise earnings."

She talked on and on and almost made it sound possible, even plausible. I didn't bother pointing out the obvious flaw. Arguing is always pointless. It's begging for trouble. And anyway, it was just one of many such ideas. Another cloud of hope, its form drifting apart before you can even see the edges. If Mom's plans have anything in common it's this: they have the substance of mist.

My head was aching by the time I finally persuaded her I needed sleep for school the next day. It was almost two in the morning and even the city's shadows looked sleepy, stretched across my floor as I flopped on my mattress.

"Night Sitta," I whispered, eyes closed. "I hope I didn't make a mistake dragging you into this mess."

He was silent, but I sensed him shuffling a little, as if he needed to rearrange himself in order to accommodate my presence in the room.

"Things probably look bad to you right now," I told him softly. "But you might as well know, it's probably going to get worse before it gets better."

Better, but not good. Never actually good.

Eight

I'd stashed the bag of office supplies in my closet and then waited a couple of days to see if Mom mentioned it. She didn't, but there was still a problem with taking it back.

The receipt wasn't in the bag. It also wasn't in the pockets of the jacket or pants she'd had on that day. There wasn't the slightest chance anyone was going to give me a refund without it and we needed that money. Badly. Enough to make me look through Mom's purse, even though my stomach feels sick when I have to do that. I'd checked her wallet to see how much cash she had and it was less than thirty bucks — at that time.

"There should be one more paycheck coming," I told Sitta as I spooned seed into his bowl after school that Friday. The truth was, I really wasn't sure. Employers all had their own systems which made it hard to keep track of Mom's pay schedules.

Sitta cocked his head and whistled. I laughed.

"Yeah, well, if there *is* another check, it sure won't be worth whistling over," I said. "But it would help."

"Call! Call!" Sitta said.

I blinked. Izelle had told me he could talk a bit, but this was the first time I'd heard him say anything that sounded like an actual word.

"Who should I call?" I asked. Sitta had no answer for that, not that I'd really expected he would.

The cage door was open and I'd put some spinach on the floor next to where I was sitting, cross-legged. So far, rummaging in the dumpster of a family-run grocery store a few blocks away had been solving the problem of getting him produce, but the birdseed wasn't going to last forever and it was a definite must. I'd also attempted to sprout a bit of popcorn and barley, but neither had worked out.

Sitta ventured out after he'd eaten some seeds. He gobbled up the slightly wilted, but well-rinsed spinach.

"You like that, huh?" I said.

"Call!" he answered.

"Believe me, pal, if there was anyone to call, I'd do it," I said.

I had the crazy thought that maybe he was trying to tell me to reach out to my dad. That might have been worth a shot if he was anywhere around, but my father works out of the country and is sometimes off the grid for weeks at a time, poking around in the ground doing whatever it is a geologist does. I think his brief taste of family life was what drove him to field work in remote locations, but in any case, he's not what you'd call accessible.

I hardly know him.

Maybe he thinks it's enough that he pays decent child support. As if that matters when things start to slide out of control and Mom wastes our money on just about anything *except* food and rent. I don't mind dumpster diving for food for Sitta, but the thought of doing it for me and Mom isn't exactly appealing.

Whatever I did or didn't have to do, calling my father obviously wasn't an option.

A quick inventory of the cupboards had told me there wasn't a chance the food we had on hand was going to last much more than a week, no matter how carefully it was rationed. Running out of food is always tough and I wasn't seeing any way around it.

It wasn't a great feeling. I'm pretty good at problem solving, but all I'd come up with this time was a headache.

So there I was, sitting, hunched over, talking to Sitta and searching my brain for an idea, when a sharp knock sounded at the door. My left foot had gone to sleep, and it prickled when I jumped up, but I hobbled over, expecting to find Mom had forgotten her key.

"Pick on any babies lately?" It was the girl from the laundry room, only without the baby, or the phone in her face.

"Every chance I get," I answered.

"In that case, I'm not sure you're the right person for the job," she said. "But I don't seem to have a lot of options. Do you want to babysit for a couple of hours?"

"Me?"

She raised an eyebrow and glanced to both sides, making the point that no one else was there.

"I meant, when?" I said.

"Now, if you can, and maybe a couple of times a week regular, if you're interested. Oh, and I'm Taylor."

"Corbin," I said. "What's the pay?" I hated to sound so mercenary, but that was obviously a detail that mattered to me.

Taylor hesitated. "My mom pays me three bucks an hour. I'll give you that."

It was lousy pay but two hours would be six bucks. Better than nothing, and it's not as if I was doing anything else. Twice a week was twelve bucks and I could make that stretch quite a ways if I had to.

"Okay," I said. Then I remembered our nearly naked apartment. "I can't do it here, though."

"Yeah, that's okay. All of Molly's stuff is at our place so you kind of need to watch her there. Can you come now?"

"I have to put my parakeet back in his cage," I said. "Which apartment are you in — I'll be there in a few minutes."

She was about to tell me when Mr. Zinbendal's door creaked open and his crabby face stuck itself into the hall.

"Keep the noise down!" he grumbled.

A lifetime of trying to keep things running smoothly had trained me to keep the peace, so I gave him a stiff nod and said nothing. Taylor, on the other hand, whirled around to face him. I could feel a cringe gathering itself together on my face when she spoke.

"Hey, Mr. Zee! Sorry about that."

And then something happened that I hadn't seen in any of *my* encounters with him. He *smiled*. Not a stingy, forced smile either. It was as though his face lit up with some kind of inner glow.

"Taylor!" he said, opening his arms. "I didn't know that was you."

I watched in disbelief as she lunged forward, threw

herself into the hug, and actually kissed his crabby old cheek.

"I can't visit now," she told him. "But I'll come see you soon."

"Wonderful, wonderful," Zinbendal said. He patted her arm before stepping back into his apartment and closing the door. For a change, he didn't practically slam it.

Taylor swung back around. She smirked, no doubt amused by my dumbfounded expression.

I switched on a blank face — another skill I've perfected over the years. If she was waiting for me to say anything, she'd be waiting a while. That's how trouble starts.

"You were going to tell me where your apartment was," I reminded her.

"We're on the ground floor," she said. "1D. First on the left."

Nine

I got to Taylor's apartment a few minutes later after catching Sitta and putting him back into his cage (with an apology and a promise I'd free him again when I returned). Taylor was waiting at the door. She had a jacket on and a pale brown satchel hung from her shoulder. It was leather, worn and cracked, and it should have looked out of place on her but somehow it didn't.

"Molly's asleep right now," she told me, already taking steps toward the door. "Her diapers and whatnot are in the bag beside the end table."

Diapers. Wet I could probably handle but ... hey, was it possible Molly pooped on some sort of schedule? Like, right after breakfast or just before bedtime, but never in the afternoon?

I couldn't ask Taylor that, obviously. She might think I'd never changed a diaper before, which, actually, I hadn't.

"When she gets up she can have the Cheerios in the

bowl on the table — she just eats them dry — and a yogurt," Taylor added, gesturing here and there. "She drinks from a sippy cup if she's thirsty — milk or water only."

"Won't she freak when she wakes up and sees a stranger?"

"Nah. She'll be fine. She's used to being around lots of people."

"But the only other time she saw me you told her I was BAD!" I reminded her.

Taylor laughed. "That's just a game to her. Don't worry."

I felt as if there were other things I should be asking, but the next minute Taylor was gone.

Molly slept for almost the first half hour I was there. On waking, she stood up in her crib and called out, "Loh! Loh!" until I got there.

As Taylor had predicted, she came to me willingly and once I'd scooped her out of bed she wrapped her arms around my neck and snuggled against me. We walked around like that for a while, until she got rest-less and started wriggling to get free. I'd only seen her in a stroller before so I didn't know if she could walk, but as soon as her feet hit the floor she was off on a wobbly sprint. She went straight to the kitchen where she pulled a chair away from the table, hauled herself up, and gave me a questioning look.

Oh, right. Snack time.

I tugged the plastic cap off the kiddie bowl and put it in front of her. She sent it flying in the few seconds it took me to get her yogurt from the fridge. Great start. I tossed the cereal that hadn't landed on the floor back into the bowl and started scooping yogurt into her mouth.

Partway through being fed, Molly remembered our meeting in the laundry room. She pointed a finger, grinned widely, and said, "BAD!" forcefully enough to send a projectile of yogurt out of her mouth and onto her pajamas. She found this hilarious and every time her amusement began to wind down she stuck her finger into it and jump-started her own giggles.

When the yogurt was gone, Molly set about eating the Cheerios, which took a while since she picked each one up and looked it over before popping it into her mouth. When she'd finally finished, she backed off the chair onto the floor and took off. I chased her down with a baby wipe and made an attempt to clean her face, hands, and pajamas. She didn't exactly cooperate.

Now that she had a full tummy (unlike me, although I'd been tempted to help myself to an apple from a bowl on the counter) she had enough energy to empty her toy box onto the floor. There was a pile of Mega Blocks in there and I helped her construct a couple of things, which she tore down as fast as I got them together.

It was a surprise when the door swung open and Taylor reappeared. It hadn't seemed at all like two hours and the big bonus was there'd been no diaper change needed.

Taylor picked Molly up and looked her over as if she was inspecting my work.

"Has she been changed?"

"I don't think she needed to be," I said. Thank goodness.

"Okay, well, here's your money," she said, passing me six bucks.

I stuffed the money into my jeans. It seemed that was the end of the conversation, since Taylor turned her back and went into the kitchen mumbling something about spaghetti. Then she spoke a bit louder.

"Say 'bye-bye' to Corbin, Molly."

Subtle. It's not like I'd planned to hang around, but that was pretty close to being told to get out.

"Bah, bah," Molly said. She stood and waved vigorously. "Baaah!"

"See you," I said. And left.

The six bucks in my pocket felt good, and the hope of making more even better, although I didn't know for sure if she wanted me to babysit again. I was thinking about what to buy with it when I opened my apartment door and saw that Mom was back. She wasn't alone.

Mike was with her and my heart sank at the thought that Mom had probably invited him for supper.

I was right. They were eating, sitting on the cushions and balancing plates on their laps. Beans with wieners chopped up in them. I walked past them, ignoring Mike's half wave, and went straight to the kitchen. Two cans of beans sat open on the cupboard and Mom had chopped a whole package of wieners into the pot with them. There was enough left for my supper, but that was it. I could have made three or four meals for me and Mom from that much food and now it was gone in one.

I scraped what was left in the pot into a bowl and was about to go to my room to eat when Mom suddenly appeared in front of me, eyes blazing.

"How *dare* you."

"What?" My strategy has always been to act innocent. Sometimes it works. Not this time.

"When there is a guest in our home, *my* guest at that, you will *not*, I repeat, *not*, behave rudely to him. Do you hear me?"

"Yes, sorry," I said. "I was just really hungry."

"You don't know what hunger is, Corbin. You have no idea. Have you ever been lying on your belly in the grass wondering —"

"You're right, Mom. I'll go apologize."

I took a step forward, but she wasn't budging.

"— and whatever exists in your mind as a good reason is, let me tell you, an uphill climb. It's an uphill climb with a cliff at the top. You understand cliffs are dangerous. People fall. They fall on their faces, sometimes people break their backs, you tell me there's a good reason for someone to break their back. Just try and make yourself believe that, buster."

That was the windup. I took a bite, but I did it slowly and without taking my eyes off Mom. You don't look away when she gets into one of her raves, which is the only way I can describe them. They go on and on and get more and more scattered — it's like watching a mirror crack and keep cracking until it's nothing more than a thousand jagged bits too small to reflect even part of an image.

"— because I've found a way. A path that no one else has had the vision to see, much less mark out for others. They're struggling, Corbin, barely able to crawl through the days and dark alleys, where things happen that should never happen to a child and all because whoever is making the rules — they want you to blame the government for everything, but there's so much more happening behind the scenes that you don't know about and I can't tell you yet, but soon I will have the whole thing exposed for the entire world to see and CEOs will be begging *me* for an appointment to learn the secret of my success, but as long as their boardrooms —"

I lifted bite after bite to my mouth, chewing, swallowing, listening without hearing, never taking my eyes off hers. Suddenly, her index finger flew toward me.

"Oh! I know! I can show you!" And with that, she rushed away, into her room.

I made a dash to the living room and plunked down on the cushion Mom had vacated. She came back seconds later, waving a sheet of paper. Mike glanced at me with a raised eyebrow.

We'd both seen Mom's "designs" before, and even someone who finds whittling cool couldn't help recognizing the nothingness of Mom's diagrams.

When she passed me the page I saw exactly what I'd been expecting. A sketch that looked like mazes superimposed over each other, along with words and anagrams that made no sense whatsoever.

"There!" Mom said triumphantly. "You see?!"

Ten

Izelle was on edge; I could see that right away.

"Look, Corbin, I don't want to be —"

I held up a hand, testing. If she gave me a chance to talk I might be able to buy more time. She didn't. She barely paused for half a second before continuing.

"It's not fair. You *promised* me and, I mean, I'm sorry your mom's been sick, but it's nearly two weeks since I saw Sitta and if you're not going to keep your end of the deal —"

She trailed off there, but it wasn't hard to figure out what would have come next.

"You're right, and I don't blame you for being upset. Things just got messed up, but you can come today if you want."

"Is your mom better?"

The true answer would have been no. She was worse, in fact. For the past week, Mom had been keeping me up half the night while she speed-talked about her so-called business plan. The details were so jumbled my exhausted brain couldn't have sorted them out if I'd tried. Which I hadn't.

I couldn't tell Izelle *that*, of course, but I did need to prepare her just in case.

"She's getting better," I lied. "In fact, some days she can manage a short walk, so she might not be there. But if she is, I've gotta warn you, the meds the doctor gave her really rev her up. If she seems kind of babbly don't worry about it."

"Sure, okay. I'm glad she's improving," Izelle said. She gave me a shaky smile. "I just miss my bird, you know?"

"Of course," I said. I didn't challenge her about calling Sitta her bird, when he was mine now.

It was a huge relief when we got to the apartment and Mom wasn't home. And there was a bonus I hadn't been expecting. Izelle had stopped on our way and bought Sitta a bag of kale and a large bunch of cilantro. But even better than that was the bag of birdseed she hauled out of her backpack.

My heart jumped when I saw that, since I was down to a few days' worth of seed. That wouldn't have been a problem if my babysitting money (eighteen bucks so far) and anything else I managed to earn only had to feed the bird, but with Mom out of work I had more than Sitta to worry about.

I felt like I should offer her something — a snack or drink or whatever, but the food supply had dwindled down to a package of frozen bagels, a few cans of soup, half a jar of applesauce, and a brownie mix that I had no eggs or oil to make. I'd thought about swiping a couple of eggs the last time I babysat Molly, but I *hate* stealing. I've taken food out of desperation a few times — but it always makes me feel like crud.

"Sorry, but we're out of bottled water," I said after I'd gone and brought out Sitta.

"That's okay," Izelle said. If she found it odd that I didn't offer her something else instead, she didn't say so.

Izelle stayed for almost an hour and I could tell Sitta was glad to see her. He showed off more than usual, prancing and cocking his head and just generally being a goof. Izelle kissed him goodbye when she was leaving and then, to my shock and horror, threw her arms around me and gave me a hug.

"Sorry," she said, laughing, when she'd let go. "I didn't mean anything by that. I'm just so happy to have seen Sitta."

"Sure," I said. "No problem."

I toasted half a bagel after she left, spread a big

spoonful of applesauce on it, and ate it as slowly as I could. Sitta marched around like a small, feathered soldier, grumbling and giving me pointed looks until I got the hint and grabbed some kale for him.

"It's not always like this," I told him. "Besides, Mom honestly can't help it when this happens to her."

Sitta let out a long low whistle.

I laughed.

"You doubt it, huh? Well, it's mostly true, but I don't blame you for getting mad at her. You should be enjoying yourself, flying around, learning new things, not worrying about when your dish is going to be filled next. I get it."

It's probably a coincidence that Sitta chose that exact moment to leave a rude deposit on the floor right beside me. But a few minutes later, he turned into a small, flying hero.

I was putting my plate in the sink when he swooped into the kitchen and landed on my shoulder. Something white was hanging from his beak and when I tugged it free I could hardly believe what I was seeing.

"Where'd you *find* this, buddy?" I asked.

He wasn't telling, but that didn't matter. What I was holding in my hand was the receipt for the bunch of office supplies Mom had brought home right after she quit her job. The bag was still tucked in the back of my closet, useless to me because I hadn't been able to find the bill of sale.

A glance at the total told me Mom had spent $46.18 on stuff she was never going to use — for a business that would never exist. That might not sound like much money if you've never been in a tight spot, but to me, at that moment in time, it was a fortune.

"Man, oh, man, Sitta," I said. "You don't know what you just did."

And then I wondered. Did he know somehow? Was it possible …?

"Stop!" I said to myself. What had just happened was a fluke. I knew that.

I hate it when my brain comes up with weird ideas and, considering the gene pool I came out of, I guess anyone would worry.

I took in a long, slow breath and let it out even slower. Sometimes that helps, but exhaustion was getting to me. I suddenly felt as though my insides had turned into a quivering mush.

Lifting my hand I gave Sitta the signal to land on my outstretched finger.

"I don't know about you, but I need sleep," I told him as his talons curled into place.

Sitta turned his head sideways, which is always partly cute and partly comical. His bright eyes glistened with what I was pretty sure was intelligence.

"Talk!" he said. Or something like that.

That seemed like good advice; everyone needs someone they can talk to. Even if that someone is a bird.

Eleven

"Corbin! Corbin!"

Mom's voice. Calling my name as she tugged at my shoulder. It took everything in me to struggle my way back to consciousness. It felt as though powerful hands were trying to pull me back into the dark emptiness of sleep.

Even when I'd forced my eyes open, my brain felt clogged and unready. I knew I'd barely drifted off before having my rest interrupted.

"Wake up!" Mom's voice was urgent but quiet, as though she was trying to whisper, but couldn't quite manage the necessary control to carry it off.

"I *can't*," I groaned. My whole body felt dog-tired and I was sure I couldn't drag myself out of bed much less spend hours listening to fragmented delusions.

"We're in danger," Mom said. "Quick, you have to get dressed. We need to get out of here."

Not that again. No, no, no.

"We're not in danger, Mom," I said. "Please just let me sleep."

"They could be here any minute," she said, as if I hadn't spoken at all. "We have no time to waste."

I sensed rather than saw her move then, a jolt, a twitch, her head snapping toward whatever had caught her attention.

"The bird," she said, standing suddenly. She moved toward Sitta as smooth as a cat and snatched the cover from his cage.

Fear shot adrenaline through my system, parting the slowly lifting fog in my brain and bringing me to my feet. I reached her side as she leaned forward, her face barely an inch from the thin bars.

"You know things, don't you?" she hissed. "You know, but you won't tell us."

"He doesn't know anything, Mom. He's just a bird," I said. Not that I really expected my words to get through.

"What I can't tell is whose side you're on," she continued, peering through the bars of his cage.

"Our side," I said firmly. "He's on our side."

Sitta's head turned slowly toward us. I could see the streetlight's soft glow reflected in his eyes as the lids slowly opened and closed. Poor guy. Now we were both losing sleep.

I scrambled into the clothes I'd dropped on the floor earlier, never taking my eyes from Mom as I dressed. She shuffled back and forth beside the cage, but made no move to open it.

"You said we had to get out of here," I reminded her once I'd tugged on my shoes. "That we were in danger?"

"Yes, danger." She nodded vigorously as her hands found each other and clasped tightly. She spun around; I wasn't sure if she was checking for someone, or if it was just a burst of energy that had to be burned up.

She grabbed my arm, pressed two fingers to her lips and then to mine, and tugged me out of my room and toward the entry door.

"Shhh," she said. She pressed her back against the wall, slid herself along, and motioned for me to do the same.

A memory flashed. A smaller version of myself, maybe six years old, on a similar late-night excursion. I remembered how my heart had pounded from the thrill of it. Tonight, I found it anything but fun.

"We'll go *up* the stairs," Mom said. "That will throw them off if they're inside already."

"What do you think they're after?" I asked.

For the record, I knew there was no "they" and I also knew going up the stairs made no sense. We'd eventually have to come back down if we were going to leave the building, and being outside is always better than skulking around the hallways. The last thing we needed in a place we'd lived for such a short time was for someone to call the police. I didn't even want to *think* about that.

What I hoped to do was get Mom talking. If that happened, there was a chance she'd distract herself from whatever had sprung up in her head and triggered her fear.

"*Me*, Corbin. They're after me, of course. I'm the one who has the formula, the plan that's going to change the way the free world treats its workers. There's a grid, and no one else realized that it's warped and twisted only I've found a way to straighten it out, but if they can get to me, they'll do everything in their power to keep me from acting on what I know."

"What if you record your plan and put it somewhere it will be protected?" I said. "Like on a USB drive in a safety deposit box at the bank."

Mom laughed, a sneering, lip-curled denunciation of my suggestion.

"They count on people being naive and gullible, falling for exactly that kind of idea. Do you know how much power these people have? There's nowhere my plan would be safe. Nowhere except right here." She tapped the side of her head.

I clenched my jaw, fighting the angry tears that were stinging my eyes. She began to move again and I went with her, followed her out the apartment door and down the hallway, up two flights of stairs, up and down the fourth-floor halls, back down one flight, through the third-floor halls and on and on. Until she decided it was safe to exit the building.

As nervous as I'd been slinking through the building, the relief I felt when we stepped into the night air disappeared fast. It was colder than I'd expected, and I wished I'd pulled a sweatshirt on under my jacket.

Tired, cold, and hungry, I trudged behind her, shivering as we crept in and around buildings. Mom paused now and then, crouching and listening. Her face was pinched and fearful and, in spite of all the miseries I had to deal with, I couldn't help pitying her. At least I knew the so-called danger wasn't real. I pulled my jacket tighter and tried to ignore the emptiness gnawing in my belly.

I don't know how long this went on. It was hours for sure, but whether it was two or five I couldn't say. It felt endless. At some point I began to stumble, half disoriented from exhaustion. Mom's terror was too powerful to let her sympathize with me. She decided I was trying to signal the enemy.

"It won't be good for you if I find out you're double-crossing me," she warned ominously.

"I swear, I'm not," I said blearily.

She was not persuaded, which actually worked in my favor because a short time later she decided we should split up and meet back at the apartment at dawn. The second I was out of her sight I beelined it home and fell into bed.

I was beyond tired, but it took a long time before I stopped shivering enough to fall back to sleep.

Twelve

I'm pretty good at forging my mom's signature, so it wasn't hard to hand in a note explaining the days I missed at school last week. Three in all. Wednesday, which was the day after Mom dragged me through the city for half the night, but also Thursday and Friday. Two nightmarish days I wish I could wipe from my memory.

Mom was in the worst state I'd ever witnessed. The ongoing terror from imagined threats to her safety had her wild-eyed and ghostly pale. She went from pacing frantically, to hunching, huddled in her room, whispering one moment, weeping the next, and sometimes crying out as though she'd been struck. The single good thing was that her fear was powerful enough to keep her from going out again.

I felt awful, watching her suffer that way. The torment she was under would have forced anyone else to shut down, but there was no escape in sleep for my mother.

I stayed as close to her as I could, and looked on helplessly. The few times I nodded off, it was for brief, fitful snatches, slumped wherever I happened to be sitting when exhaustion overcame me.

Finally, mercifully, Mom crashed around dawn on Saturday and we both slept the day away. Sunday was quiet and I could hardly wait to get out of the apartment and back to school on Monday. With my forged excuse claiming I'd been sick with an infected throat.

My homeroom teacher, Mr. Cameron, didn't comment on the note, but when I was leaving at the end of the day he asked me how I was feeling.

"A lot better," I said. I tried to meet his eyes, but couldn't quite manage it.

That was because his voice sounded as if he was actually *concerned*. Without warning I realized I was in danger of crying. Stress and fatigue can do that to you, even if you've learned to be tough, which I definitely have.

"Well, let me know if there's anything you need," he said. "Anything at all. I mean it."

So. He'd finally gotten around to looking at my file. Terrific.

"Sure. Thanks."

I got out of there quick and spent a minute hauling

in oxygen while I rummaged around in my locker for nothing.

As soon as I'd smoothed out I started home, although I had one stop to make first. That was the grocery store, the one with the dumpster where I'd been getting discarded produce for Sitta. I got caught the last time I'd gone there, but when I explained it was for my parakeet the guy had been nice about it.

"We had budgies when I was a kid," he said, grinning at the memory. "They were quite the characters. I'd like to have a bird or two now, but my wife doesn't like them."

He asked a few questions about Sitta and then went inside and came back with a bag of dried stuff like beans, lentils, rice, and barley. There was a piece of tape over a spot that had been punctured.

"For sprouting," he said.

"I tried that a couple of times," I admitted. "I didn't have much luck."

He got me to describe my failed efforts and gave me some pointers of things I could do differently, including how to make sure air was able to circulate — something I hadn't done in my previous attempts.

I thanked him. Then, on a whim, I said, "I'm a pretty good worker if you ever need help with odd jobs."

"I can't think of anything at the moment," he said. "But check back with me in a day or two."

That was my reason for stopping there on my way home from school today, but when I looked inside there was a woman behind the counter. I walked up and down the street a couple of times, snatching quick glances through the window as I passed by, but there was no sign of the guy. I decided I'd try again tomorrow.

I set my jaw and started to walk home. Even though I knew better than to *ever* count on anything, disappointment sat in my gut like a stone. There was almost nothing left to eat in the apartment. I'd spent the last three bucks I had on a half-price loaf of bread and a can of tuna yesterday and I had no idea where I was going to get more cash.

My babysitting job had gone down the drain last Thursday when Taylor came to my place to ask if I could watch Molly. At that particular moment, the only thing I could do was shake my head "no" and ease the door shut — before she could hear Mom's barely coherent mutterings about big corporations and the miserable, sniveling traitors at her last job.

For a few minutes I'd stood, slumped silently against the door frame. Even without seeing her, I knew Taylor was still there in the hallway. I'd half expected she'd knock again and demand to know what was wrong with me. She hadn't and eventually I heard her walking away. Safe to assume that was the end of that job and the bit of money I'd been earning from it. Twelve bucks a week. Food on the table.

I turned onto my street wondering about Mom's state of mind today. She'd been calmer and close to quiet yesterday. That might have been exhaustion, or it could mean she was coming down.

I let myself hope. It wasn't impossible that she'd smoothed out. Not happy, but steadier. She could even have realized that we were out of food and gone to the food bank. They won't give me anything, but the few times Mom has gone there we've gotten a bunch of stuff — peanut butter, Cheez Whiz, bread, pasta, potatoes, carrots, cereal, milk, canned goods …

I felt my stomach clench and forced myself to stop thinking about food. I kicked at a stray stone on the sidewalk. The cold air stung my eyes.

My apartment building was cold and gray against the fading sky and the sight of it sent a sudden shiver through me. Dismal seemed to be the only constant in my life.

I trudged toward the doorway too preoccupied to notice Izelle standing there until it was too late. She saw me first and for a second I thought she might come charging at me like some kind of enraged bull, that's how furious she looked. It took everything in me to keep walking toward her.

"Hey!" I said as I got closer. I lifted my hand in a casual, friendly wave, trying frantically to figure out what I'd done wrong. Not that I doubted she'd fill me in.

"Liar!" she said when I was a few feet away.

What? *Liar?*

What had I lied about? I tried to remember if I'd even talked to her today. She parked her hands on her hips, thrust her face toward me, and cleared up the mystery as I got closer.

"Last week you said I could come every Monday. You promised. And then you didn't even come home after school."

It sounded vaguely familiar. Not that I thought she was making it up, but so much had happened in the last few days.

"Oh, man! Look, I'm sorry. I had to go somewhere after school and I just forgot, but come on up and have a visit."

Izelle gave me a thin smile. I returned something that was probably closer to a grimace, but she was too relieved to mind.

"It's okay — sorry I yelled at you."

Whatever else, it was a relief to get out of the cold. We made our way up the stairs and down the hall to my apartment. I heard Zinbendal's door creak open just as I pulled mine shut behind us.

I breathed out slowly, relieved that there was no sign of Mom.

Thirteen

I noticed I didn't like watching Sitta with Izelle.

Sure, I expected Sitta to be happy to see her. He'd been her bird for more than a year. And he wasn't the problem in any case. It was her. There was an attitude of ownership in the way she talked to him and leaned her head in his direction and gave me completely unnecessary advice.

"He likes it when you do this," she said, like she was offering up an amazing secret. Except, what she was showing me was how she stroked his feathers, and it was the exact same way I've done it since he got here, without her instructions. There aren't a lot of different ways you can pat a bird.

She talked about his favorite foods too, and I hated the way it came across like a criticism. It was as if she knew I hadn't been able to get him certain things, even though I acted like he was eating them on a daily basis. No matter what she mentioned, I made myself grin and say things like, "Oh, yeah, he goes crazy for that stuff," as if I got it for him all the time.

The thought strayed through my mind that we'd soon be kicked out of here and I'd be switching to yet another school and these visits would be over with. Which should have brought a flood of relief, even in anticipation. It didn't.

"Okay, well, I'd better get going," Izelle said after a long half hour. She carried Sitta into my room, to his cage, and kissed his beak before inserting him inside and shutting the door. I decided to wait in the hall. When she came out she paused by the kitchen entrance.

"Doing some sprouting for our bird, huh?" she said.

Our bird?

I let that go, not wanting to slow down her departure. But she'd stepped into the kitchen and picked up the bag of dried things I was using to grow sprouts.

"Nice mix," she said. "This will last him a long time, unless, of course, you're planning to make soup."

She laughed at her own joke, and I managed to get out a "heh-heh" too, but her words almost made my knees give out.

How had I missed that? I'd so completely related that bag of dried beans and peas and barley, and a dozen other things, as sprouting material for Sitta that its intended use had never once crossed my mind. It was *soup mix*, not bird food!

As soon as the door shut behind Izelle, I raced back to the kitchen and read the instructions on the bag. There wasn't much to it and while I didn't have any of the other ingredients they suggested, I couldn't have cared less. I half filled a pot with water, rinsed a cupful of the mix, and put it on to cook. As soon as it started to boil, I turned it down and put the lid on, then started to look for things I could add to the water for flavor.

I came up with onion powder, chili flakes, oregano, and some celery seed. After measuring in a spoonful of each, I added salt and pepper. It was even starting to smell good. And better than that, the thought that I'd soon be filling my empty stomach with a warm bowl of soup somehow gave me courage. I double-checked that it was simmering on the lowest setting and wouldn't need any attention for a while, then I slipped out of the apartment.

A moment later I stood at Taylor's door. I knocked before I had a chance to talk myself out of it, but it wasn't Taylor who opened the door. It was some guy.

"What?" he said.

I blinked.

"Who is it, DJ?" came Taylor's voice from the background.

"Who knows?" the guy said over his shoulder. "Some weirdo who's just standing here not saying anything."

"I uh —" I began. That was when Taylor's head poked itself between DJ and the door frame.

"Oh. Corbin," she said, monotone.

I'd gone there to explain, or actually, to offer a lie about my odd behavior last week, hoping, of course, I might get the babysitting job back. This obviously wasn't the right time for that — if a right time was even possible.

"Did you want something?" Taylor asked.

"Oh, uh, yeah," I said. "I was wondering if I could borrow some ketchup."

Taylor stared for a silent second or two.

"You came here to borrow ketchup," she echoed. It wasn't exactly a question, but I nodded anyway. Probably much more vigorously than I needed to.

Her head withdrew. A moment later it reappeared, this time accompanied by her hand, thrust forward, holding a ketchup bottle that was about one quarter full.

"You can keep it," she said. "We have another bottle."

I took it. I mumbled a thoroughly embarrassed thanks and started toward the stairs. Behind me, I heard DJ muttering something that was probably rude and probably about me, although I couldn't actually make out the details. The door closed.

Back in my apartment I checked on my soup and went to let Sitta back out of his cage. It wasn't until half an hour later that I noticed Mom's purse, slumped in the corner of the kitchen.

A tickle crept up my neck.

Mom was home? Had she been home the whole time, or was it possible she'd come in while I was at Taylor's place, accidentally borrowing ketchup?

I crept toward her door, which was closed tightly. I stood there for I don't know how long, listening.

Finally, with growing dread, I tapped.

"Mom?"

Silence. I tapped again.

"Mom? Are you in there?"

Nothing. I tapped a little louder.

"Mom? Are you okay?"

When there was still nothing on the other side of the door but silence, I opened it and stepped inside. The curtains were drawn, but a thin beam of sunlight cast an eerie glow over the room. It did little to illuminate the small figure on the mattress in the corner. A sheet was drawn up to my mother's chin. She was lying absolutely still.

I reached for the light switch, but drew my hand back without flicking it on. Instead, I crept closer and peered down.

"MOM!"

Her eyes remained closed, but her mouth parted enough to breathe out three words.

"Leave me alone."

My gut revolted in some weird combination of relief and rebellion. I barely made it to the toilet in time.

Fourteen

The soup didn't have a lot of flavor. I didn't care. I'd gobbled down half a bowl when it occurred to me to stir in a squirt of the ketchup. That improved the taste a bit, but the best thing was how amazing it felt to have a full stomach. There was still a fair amount left too, and if I needed to I could make at least two more pots from what was left in the bag of dried beans and stuff.

I made a mental note that, from now on when I buy food, I'll get more of it, plus oatmeal, which can go a long way, even if you have to eat it without milk or sugar. I usually get oatmeal, but somehow I'd forgotten it when I spent the refund from the office supplies.

I took some soup to Mom after I'd eaten, but she refused to take so much as a single bite. I dumped it back in the pot and left a glass of water on the floor beside her mattress.

"Let me know if you want anything later," I told her.

My voice sounded strangely loud in the silence of her room.

I stepped into the hall, tugged her door closed, and went to find Sitta. He was in my room but he hopped onto my shoulder and stayed there until we got to the living room. As I dropped down onto a cushion, he rose into the air, made a wide circle above me, then flew down the hall and back. I smiled when he picked the other cushion to land on. It's become his favorite spot, probably because of the splashes of color in it.

"Well, buddy," I told him, "I'm afraid it looks like this could be a bad one. You don't know her well yet, but when Mom comes out of the wild-ideas, awake-for-days phase, she usually drops, and the faster she drops, the harder it is for her to get back up."

"Go! Go!" Sitta said. Then he added something that sounded like, "What?"

"I don't blame you for wondering," I said. "It can get really scary. Sometimes it seriously looks like she's going to stop breathing because it's too much effort and she doesn't care if she keeps on or not."

Sitta let that sink in without commenting, but I continued. It felt good to talk about it, even if it was just to a bird.

"It won't last forever. It could be days, or it could be

a lot longer, but eventually, she'll come out of it. Then she's okay for a while. Usually a few months. Once it was longer, when she stayed on her meds. But it always starts over.

"It doesn't have to affect you though, buddy," I added quickly.

"Call!" said Sitta. "Who? Who?"

He was right. There was no one to call.

"So if I seem distracted now and then," I explained, "it's just that I'm *always* on edge, waiting. Whatever's happening at the moment? It never lasts. That makes it hard to relax and enjoy it when things are good."

Sitta gnawed a bit at the feathers on his left side.

"I *hate* it," I said.

Sitta cocked his head at my angry tone. I won't say he looked shocked exactly, but there was puzzlement in the way his face was tilted.

"Don't get me wrong. I love my mother, but it's hard, the way life is with her. And I try to protect her, but there's only so much I can do, or hide. I know, for example, that old Mr. Zinbendal across the hall has been hearing things. And that old geezer has troublemaker written all over him."

Sitta dropped an oystery splotch on the cushion and flew back down the hall.

"Good talk!" I called after him.

I'd just finished cleaning Sitta's cushion deposit when Taylor knocked at the door. I knew it was her before I went to answer by the sharp, four-rap pattern.

"So," she said as soon as I opened the door. "What did you *really* want earlier?"

I'd been ready with a story to tell her at that time, but like most lies it refused to reassemble itself on the spot. I edged uneasily toward the truth.

"Just to say I was sorry I couldn't babysit last week," I said. "I didn't want you to think I meant to quit altogether — if you still need me sometime."

"I didn't think you were quitting," she said.

"Oh. Well, good then."

Taylor sniffed the air and wrinkled her nose. "What's that weird smell?"

"I made soup."

"In that case, remind me to never eat your cooking. It smells like mouthwash."

"It — oh *that*. I was cleaning a cushion. Sitta had an accident."

That seemed to amuse her. "Sorry," she said, an apology that would have looked more sincere if she'd stopped grinning. But then her forehead scrunched up quizzically.

"You didn't mean you actually *made* soup, right?"

"Sure I did," I said, as if I'd been doing it all my life.

Taylor's eyes narrowed suspiciously.

"*Homemade* soup?" she said.

"Yup."

I don't know why she thought I might lie about soup, but she clearly didn't believe me. It probably had something to do with my skill at projecting nervousness.

"Show me," she demanded.

"Show you?" I felt my face getting warm. "What, you've never seen soup before?"

"I've never seen soup *you* made before. What, are you, embarrassed? How bad could it be?"

"It's not all that great," I admitted.

But Taylor was moving forward, and was inside the apartment before I had time to think of a reason to keep her out. She'd made it halfway through the living room before coming to a dead stop and whirling around to face me.

"Where are all your things? Are you guys moving out?"

That was when something malfunctioned. I'm not sure if it was my brain or mouth or possibly both, but when I tried to repeat the lie I'd told Izelle about us being minimalists, it got distorted en route.

"No. We're minibalistics."

"You're *what*?" Taylor said.

"We don't like to have a bunch of stuff," I explained.

"You mean you're minimalists?" she asked after a second or two.

"That's what I said," I claimed.

"Oh-kaaay," she said. After another look around she remembered why she'd come in and headed toward the kitchen.

I followed helplessly as she trounced her way to the stove where the pot still sat. Her hand darted out and snatched the lid off like she was about to expose me as a big fraud.

For the next minute or so she stood, leaning forward and peering into the pale mix. Maybe it took her that long to decide whether what she was looking at could actually be called soup. When she straightened up and swung around to face me, I was braced for some sarcasm and insults. So what she said was a surprise.

"Looks better than I expected. Although, I didn't actually come by to inspect your," she paused and smirked, "uh, culinary accomplishments. I wanted to know if you could babysit tomorrow."

"Sure," I told her. "Right after school?"

"Yes. And the next couple of days too, if you can."

"Yeah, no problem."

"Great," she said. "Oh, and I keep forgetting to mention this but help yourself to anything you want to eat whenever you're watching Molly. That's Mom's rule for all our babysitters."

She left then, and I went in search of Sitta, who was on the windowsill in our room.

"We're in the money, buddy," I told him. "Eighteen bucks coming our way!"

Sitta played it cool about the news of our wealth. I didn't care. I couldn't stop smiling.

I still had the babysitting job, and tomorrow when I was done watching Molly, I'd see if the guy from the store was around and ask him about odd jobs. Even with Mom in her current state, it seemed that things were looking up.

"You know what?" I told Sitta. "I think you're good luck. Maybe you can put a spell on Mom and make her better."

"Foo!" said Sitta.

Fifteen

I like to fly well under the radar at school. That isn't hard as long as I do my work and stay out of trouble. If Mom happens to be doing okay when parent-teacher meetings come along, fine. But if she's not, I make sure I haven't given my teacher any reason to get in touch with her.

Another thing I don't do is make friends, which I realize makes me sound antisocial. I'm not. I just don't want anyone asking questions, noticing things, or inviting me places I can't afford to go, which is basically anywhere that costs money.

Besides the potential for prying, there's just no point starting friendships that will only last as long as it takes for us to get kicked out of our apartment. Then Mom wants out of that neighborhood altogether, which is never a problem in a city this size. I've hinted more than a few times that I wouldn't mind finishing a full year at the same school, but every time we've relocated it's been far enough to make that impossible.

So I don't start things, I *avoid* them. In most cases I will walk away from trouble even if it makes me look like a gutless wimp. Today was an exception and, even with what happened, I can't help feeling that somehow it wasn't exactly my fault. Unless I can be blamed for not spotting a bully who's a couple of inches shorter than me and, to quote Mom's friend Mike, looks like he couldn't fight his way out of a wet paper bag.

Not that most bullies want to fight — unless there's a small army to help them. Like I said, I try to keep my distance from trouble but I've seen enough of that sort to know most of them are actually cowards with a capital C. I guess everyone knows that.

The difference is, a lot of them *look* tough enough to throw down, even if they almost never do unless they're cornered. Not this guy. Mack something or other. He looked about as threatening as a hamster.

I had no lunch with me, so I was wandering, killing time and avoiding the smells and sounds of food. I'd just passed the science lab when Mack came around the corner and our right shoulders bumped. The kind of thing anyone who wasn't a moron would ignore.

Unfortunately, Mack didn't fit that description.

"Who do you think you are?" he demanded.

I switched my expression to neutral and started to sidestep him, which he misread as weakness. A bully's courage rises with every sign that a target fears him.

"Where do you think you're going?" he said. A brilliant probe for pointless information.

I *still* would have let it go — the hostility-for-nothing, the tough-guy attitude. There wasn't a single thought in my head of making any kind of deal out of it.

And then he grabbed my arm.

That's where it got weird. I can't even say what happened to me, or why. The classic explanation would be that I snapped, but it felt like more than a snap. An explosion, maybe, an eruption of epic proportions.

Almost before I knew what was happening, I had him backed up against the wall and was yelling into his terrified face.

I don't know what all I said, although even in my crazed state I was aware that some of what I was shouting at him was complete babble. No doubt that added to his shock and fear.

This went on for, I don't know, a minute? Maybe two or three? Until a small audience had formed and someone — a couple of guys actually — hauled me away from him.

For the record, I hadn't hit him, or done anything else to actually hurt him. Still, the way he sank to the floor where he curled up and started whimpering, you'd think for sure he'd been hammered good and hard.

"What's your problem?" I yelled, although not as loud or angry.

Mack's head lifted enough for him to level a look of pure loathing at me. "He's crazy!" he screamed. "Get him out of here!"

"Not so tough now, are you?" I said. But all the fire and fury had drained out of me. Good thing, because by then a teacher was hurrying toward us.

As I was escorted toward the main office, the sound of running feet caught my attention and when I turned my head, there was Izelle, falling in beside me. She said nothing, but she walked along with me all the way to the office doorway and as the teacher motioned me inside, I heard Izelle say, "It will be okay, Corbin."

I gave her a nod, wondering how such a small gesture could have felt so important.

A few minutes later I was in the principal, Ms. Delvecchio's, office. She used some heavy pauses and disappointed looks to convey her disapproval of what I'd just done. On the other hand, she told me she knew every conflict had two sides and if I wanted to share mine she'd certainly listen.

I said nothing. Not just because I didn't want to be a rat, but because there was no way to spin what had happened in my favor. How could I justify the way I'd come so unhinged over being asked a couple of dumb questions and having my arm grabbed?

I didn't understand it myself.

That mattered a lot less than the fact that I *did* understand what was going to happen next. This was confirmed before many more minutes had passed when Ms. Delvecchio informed me I was being suspended.

"Your mother will need to come in for a meeting before we can allow you to return to class."

Since we had no phone, she told me, a letter would be sent to Mom with the details of this appointment.

"As for the rest of today," Ms. Delvecchio continued, "you'll go to the in-school suspension program."

In-school suspension is a concept I don't quite get, but I gathered my stuff and reported there. Four other students were sprawled at desks, supposedly giving at least a little attention to the work in front of them. The teaching assistant on duty motioned me to a seat and told me to find something productive to do.

I hauled out my math homework, but it was impossible to concentrate when all I could think about was how badly I'd messed up, and how one stupid outburst had earned me problems I might not be able to fix.

Unless she had some kind of remarkable bounce-back, my mother wasn't going to be coming to any meeting. And a forged note wouldn't help in this situation.

Unfortunately, she was all I had. Unless you count my father. Which I don't.

By the time school ended for the afternoon I'd spent some time thinking about that. My father. Payer of support, ignorer of son.

The fury I'd felt toward Mack earlier apparently hadn't worked itself entirely out of my system, because on my way home I stopped at the library and sent my so-called father an email. I decided it was time he heard what I thought of him.

Sixteen

The letter from my school got here yesterday. Our meeting with Ms. Delvecchio is supposed to be on Thursday morning. Two days from now.

I'd opened the letter myself since Mom is still lying in bed, spending most of the time sleeping or staring at the ceiling. She's had a bit of food — on Saturday I went to the bakery and forced myself to spend a little over four bucks of my babysitting money on some of Mom's favorite treats. A brownie, a lemon bar, and a couple of date-filled oatmeal cookies.

I took the box home, cut off the string they'd tied it with, and put it and a fork on the floor beside her mattress. I hoped the smells would get to her and sure enough she's been taking nibbles, working her way through them a bit at a time. It's not great nutrition, but I guess it's better than nothing. And she's been drinking water, so that's good too.

I watch daily for signs that she's coming out of this.

By now, I know what to look for. Nothing yet. I remind myself over and over that it won't last forever no matter how bad it seems.

These days and weeks have always been the worst. The silence gets so huge it's almost enough to crush you. But this time, I'm not one hundred percent alone.

Sitta has proven to be a great listener, easily as good as a dog. Although, I've got to say he looked pretty startled when I filled him in on something that happened when I was in grade four. (To be honest, he looks startled a lot. It's kind of his go-to expression.)

"That was the time she just disappeared," I told him, remembering the crawling panic I'd felt looking for her. Wondering. "And I don't know what made me think of it, but on the second day I checked our storage locker in the basement. We didn't have anything to store, but I remembered the landlord showing it to us, and giving Mom a key."

Sitta strutted back and forth on his cushion. It looked like he was impatient to hear more, which brought a grin to my face.

"So, anyway, I went to the locker and at first I thought I was at the wrong one because there were all these cardboard boxes in it and, like I said, ours was empty. But it was ours all right. And Mom was in there, hidden by all this cardboard."

My throat got tight, reliving the moment when I'd seen her, crouched down, trembling and whimpering like a frightened animal.

"Nothing I said could convince her to come out. Luckily, that was one of the rare times when my father happened to be around, so I got a hold of him and he came over. As soon as he saw Mom, he called for an ambulance.

"Then he sent me upstairs to wait for him in the apartment," I said. I'd been only too happy to obey. Who wants to see their mother hiding like that?

"I was watching out the window when they took her. They had Mom strapped to a stretcher and it bothered me for a long time, thinking about her being tied down. I didn't know until a lot later they secure all patients that way, to keep them safe."

"Foo! Foo!" said Sitta. He hopped down to the floor and walked around behind the cushion. I tried not to let my imagination go off the rails, but it honestly *looked* like the story was upsetting him.

"Sorry, buddy, but I've gotta tell you the rest. See, the worst part was, even with the window closed I could hear these awful screams coming from her. Pain and terror and rage."

I could almost still hear those sounds, and it's been making me wonder if maybe I sounded like that last week when I lost it with Mack. Could that be a sign I'm going to follow in my mother's unsteady footsteps?

That creeps into my brain a lot. What if I have this too? I've seen the pain of it from the outside. How much worse would it be to have those slithering thoughts crawling through my own head?

"I can't imagine anything more terrifying," I whispered. And then, because I didn't *want* to imagine it, I forced myself to think about something else.

"We're pretty good for food right now," I told Sitta proudly. Not only had I babysat Molly three afternoons last week, but the guy at the grocery store made me a great deal. For helping with some cleaning for an hour a couple of times a week, he loads me up with produce that's starting to droop, for Sitta, and he lets me take ten bucks worth of anything else I want. Between that and the babysitting money, things are looking pretty good.

There's a brand-new jar of peanut butter, two full loaves of bread (one in the freezer to stay fresh), macaroni, oatmeal, canned beans, and eggs in the fridge and cupboards right this minute. I can fix myself something to eat anytime I want.

On the other hand, the end of the month is almost here and that means the rent will be due. Mom usually has to pay first and last when we move, but I'm not sure exactly how it all works when you get behind. If she's back on her feet soon, and gets a job right away, maybe she'll be able to catch up and we can stay. That's happened a few times in the past, but a lot depends on the landlord.

"You know what we could use, Sitta?" I asked him after I'd explained our situation. "A miracle. Got anything like that tucked in those feathers of yours?"

That's when Sitta lifted both wings, spreading them out at his sides as if he was about to take off. Except, he didn't. He flapped them once or twice, dipped his head and lifted it back up looking straight at me.

"Spell! Spell!" he called.

"You casting a spell, buddy?" I said. And I laughed.

Because at that moment it seemed amusing.

Seventeen

It was that same night, just before three in the morning, when something woke me.

I was instantly alert, although I didn't move for a minute or two. Instead, I lay there, listening hard. Beside me, Sitta's cage made a gravestone-shaped silhouette against the light coming through the window.

I'd almost convinced myself that whatever had disturbed me must have crept in from beyond the walls of the apartment. A single, sudden noise that had faded before I'd fully wakened. My mind began to relax back toward sleep, which is when the silence was broken by a sound I couldn't quite identify. It was definitely coming from inside the apartment. A cross between a cough and a gurgle. And something else. Something else …

Shrugging off my blanket, I got up, pulled on my jeans, and tiptoed to the doorway. It came again, the sound that didn't belong. Only quieter this time, like an echo.

Like it was muffled.

A jolt of heat ran through me. I crossed the hall to Mom's room, turned the doorknob and pushed on the door in one movement. It barely budged.

"Mom!" I said, somehow managing to keep my voice steady. "Mom?"

She made a sound — low and wordless. A sinking away sound.

And I could already smell something through the sliver of space the door had opened.

Vomit.

I knew what that meant. And I knew why she'd jammed things under the door to keep it from opening.

I pushed harder, gaining an inch or two, but not enough to squeeze through. I shoved with all my strength, saying, "Let me in, please. Come on, just let me in for a minute."

I could see her face, ghostly pale, turned slightly toward me on the pillow, staring vacantly. I pleaded again and I kept pushing, but the door held firm.

And then, with a movement that seemed to take every bit of effort she could summon, my mother grasped the blanket and pulled it up and over her face. Like a corpse. I took a step back and threw myself against her door. It didn't budge.

I knew I had an emergency on my hands, but oddly

what I most wanted to do in that moment was crumple helplessly into a ball on the floor. The urge was so powerful it was all I could do to stay on my feet and force myself to focus on what had to be done. Because my mother needed help immediately and there was no one else who could make sure she got it.

This was a situation where seconds counted. And so, a few heartbeats later, I found myself pounding on Mr. Zinbendal's door, yelling, "Help! We need help."

I was still saying it when the door opened a few inches and his frightened face appeared.

"You!" he said. "What is it?"

"Call 911!" I cried. "My mom needs an ambulance."

Zinbendal didn't hesitate. He crossed the floor to a table and picked up the receiver of some kind of old-fashioned phone. He flicked on a dim lamp and pressed three buttons. As he waited for someone to answer he turned sideways and motioned me into the apartment.

The place was like a museum of old furniture, all oversized. There were big square tables, enormous chairs, and the bulkiest couch I've ever seen. I made my way in and stopped in the middle of the room. By then, Zinbendal was telling the emergency operator the address.

"I don't *know* what's wrong with her," he said after

a pause. "Someone comes to my door looking for help this time of night — I don't ask a lot of questions."

He shot me a questioning look, eyebrows raised and free hand stretched forward.

"She's sick and, uh, trapped in her room," I said. And then, because I was afraid that might not sound urgent enough, I added, "I think she took too much medicine by mistake."

Zinbendal let that sink in for a second or two before he spoke into the phone again. "It sounds like an overdose," he said.

I edged back to the doorway while he was listening to the operator. As he glanced over at me, I lifted a hand, said, "Thanks a lot. Sorry for disturbing you," and slipped back across the hall to my own place.

I left our apartment door unlocked for the emergency workers, but before they arrived it opened and Mr. Zinbendal stepped in. He spied me down the hall outside Mom's room and came shuffling toward me. I saw that he'd put on slippers and hauled a housecoat on over his pajamas.

He paused as he made his way through the living room. I watched him taking in the emptiness of the place, but when he spoke he didn't mention the lack of furnishings.

"Is there anything I can help with while we wait?" he asked.

"Not unless you can talk my mom into opening her door," I said.

He looked unsure, but came forward and stood near the narrow opening. "Your son here is very worried about you, ma'am. Can you clear the door to reassure him?"

Apparently, reassuring me wasn't one of Mom's priorities just then. But Mr. Zinbendal gave it a shot.

"It appears your mother has thrown up," he said softly. "That seems hopeful, as she may have expelled some of whatever she took."

And he patted my arm.

His response to my middle-of-the-night plea for help and the kindness in his voice and actions seemed strange considering how crabby he'd been since we moved into this place. And he'd probably go right back to his usual self once the crisis was over. That didn't matter. I was just glad not to be standing there alone, hoping my mother didn't die before help arrived.

The EMTs, a man and a woman, came minutes later, moving quickly without running. They managed to get her door open by pushing and pulling it to loosen what was jammed underneath, and then shoving it out of the way. They hurried to Mom's side, removing the blanket she'd covered herself with a short time earlier.

Her eyes were closed and she was very still.

Mr. Zinbendal tried to shield me from seeing what was going on, but I sidestepped him and watched as one of the paramedics knelt, pressing fingers against Mom's neck.

I watched, and I heard.

I heard him say, "There's no pulse."

Eighteen

Everything in me wanted to rush to my mother's side. Three things stopped me.

One was knowing if I got in the way, I'd end up somewhere that I couldn't even see what was happening. The second was Mr. Zinbendal's surprisingly firm hand on my shoulder.

"You need to stay clear to let them do their work," he said.

The third reason, I don't want to talk about.

I'll say this. They definitely knew what they were doing. You never saw two people work so fast or efficiently. It was apparent by their slick movements and the concise way they communicated that they knew exactly what needed to be done and weren't wasting any time about it. While that went on, I mostly watched my mother's face. Zinbendal's hand stayed on my shoulder and that helped keep me calm more than I can explain.

Someone told me later it was less than three minutes before they pulled her back to the land of the living. Which meant, of course, that she'd actually been dead, and would still be dead if they hadn't gotten there on time. My mother.

It had felt a lot longer than a few minutes, watching, waiting, almost not breathing myself until her body jerked for the second time, in response to the defibrillator, and I heard the female paramedic say, "Okay, we've got a beat."

It took a while after that for them to decide she was stable enough to move to the ambulance. During that time Mr. Zinbendal disappeared. When I saw he was gone I assumed he'd headed back to bed, but just as they were wheeling out the stretcher he reappeared, dressed in street clothes and wearing a jacket and boots.

"I imagine you'll want to go along to the hospital and see how she's doing," he said. "I've called a cab and it will be here in a few minutes, so get ready quick."

I slipped on my shoes and jacket and the two of us went downstairs to wait. It didn't take long before a taxi pulled up and ten minutes later we were getting out at the hospital. The fare was almost sixteen dollars, which made my stomach clench, especially when I remembered there'd be a return trip to pay for too.

"I'll make sure my mom pays you back," I said as we made our way in through the sliding glass doors of the emergency department.

I'd taken a half dozen steps before I realized Mr. Zinbendal had stopped in his tracks. I turned and went back to find out why.

"I don't know your name," he said as I reached him. "What is it?"

"Corbin."

"Now look here, Corbin," he said. "I don't want you or your mom worrying about a few dollars spent on a cab. So let's settle that right now. This is a favor. Someday, maybe I'll need a hand with something and you'll do me a good turn too, but in the meantime, no one *owes* me anything. Understood?"

I couldn't speak, but I nodded. And then something broke loose inside me and the next thing I knew I was holding onto him and bawling like a little kid.

For a couple of minutes we stood there, Zinbendal awkwardly patting my shoulder while I tried to bury my head in the stale-smelling folds of his long, gray coat. Shame scalded my neck and face, leaving deep red blotches that only subsided when I detached myself and snuck off to the washroom where I patted cold water over them again and again.

He was waiting in the hall just outside the washroom when I emerged. We walked in silence toward a nurse who was sitting at a desk with high sides. Mr. Zinbendal explained that my mother had just been brought in by ambulance.

"Your mother's name?" the nurse asked me.

"Rhea Hayes," I said.

She disappeared for a moment. When she returned, she told us, "Doctor Scaria is with her now. You can go ahead — she's in the second room on the left down that corridor."

Mr. Zinbendal asked if I wanted him to come with me or stay in the waiting area.

"You can come," I said, trying to sound like it didn't matter when even the thought of walking in there alone was terrifying. If I'd had to, I could have — would have. But I *didn't* have to go by myself and that felt kind of amazing.

Mom was hooked up to monitors and an IV. I looked for a sign that she was glad to be alive, maybe even glad to see me, but there was nothing. Not a flicker of anything that would make you think the brain operating her reactions so much as recognized who I was or what was going on.

Dr. Scaria greeted us with a smile and a handshake.

She said Mom was stable, but she'd have to stay in hospital for a while. When she learned that Mr. Zinbendal was just a neighbor, Dr. Scaria asked if there was a relative I could stay with until my mother's emergency contact could make arrangements for me.

I almost blurted that my father wasn't even in the country. Not the kind of mistake I'd ever have made if I wasn't so stressed. Luckily, I caught myself in time and managed to nod, probably harder than necessary.

"Oh, sure," I said.

"I'll see to it," Mr. Zinbendal added. An unexpected ally, I thought, until I realized he meant it.

The doctor seemed satisfied.

"Your mom will be sent up to ICU and closely monitored for the next twenty-four hours," she said. "After that, she'll be transferred to the Psych Unit."

The last time Mom was in Psych, I ended up in a foster home for almost a month. My foster mother, Mrs. Jenkins, was an older woman who thought her job was to watch me like a hawk every minute I wasn't in school or asleep. She dutifully brought me to see Mom three times a week — on a schedule she'd worked out and stuck to like her senior's discount might be revoked if she didn't. Mrs. Jenkins was awfully fond of her senior's discount. I don't think she was quite as fond of me, probably because I kept lying to her and she kept catching me at it.

That had been a long month and I had no intention of going through another one like it. Especially since I was two years older now and perfectly capable of taking care of myself. Besides, I couldn't risk losing my jobs, just in case we didn't get kicked out of the apartment. Most importantly, I needed to be home to take care of Sitta.

On the cab ride home I starting working on a plan to trick Mr. Zinbendal into thinking someone was looking after me. I hated to lie to him when he'd come through in such a big way, but I had no choice.

That's what I assumed anyway. Until I got back to the apartment and, after some effort, persuaded Mr. Zinbendal that I'd be fine alone for what was left of the night.

"I'll just get some sleep and contact one of my relatives in the morning," I told him. One of my fictitious relatives.

"And thank you so much for everything you did tonight," I added. That seemed to need more than words so, lame as it was, I stuck out my hand.

He shook it solemnly and told me I was very welcome and he was glad we were friends now. I didn't answer that, because I couldn't.

I was trying to decide whether I'd invent an aunt or an uncle when I stepped into the apartment and nearly jumped out of my skin.

Seated on one of the living room cushions, a man's dark gray shadow was slumped against the far wall.

Nineteen

"Dad?"

As the shadow stirred and straightened I realized that of course it wasn't my father, which made me feel foolish. I should have known better than to hope for his help. He hadn't even bothered to answer the angry email I'd sent, much less show up in my actual life.

My hand went to the light switch and flicked it on.

Mom's friend Mike blinked, lifted a hand to shield his eyes, squinted, and said, "Corbin."

"What are *you* doing here?" I said. It came out sounding rude, but I hadn't meant it that way. It was disappointment, because he wasn't my father, mysteriously arriving to save the day and act like he, as Mom would say, gave a flying Fig Newton about me.

"The hospital called me," he answered, getting to his feet and stretching.

"Why would they call you?"

"Your mom has me listed as her emergency contact,"

he said. "They called to let me know what happened tonight."

I let that sink in.

"Okay, but what are you doing *here*?" By then my hostility was more forced than felt. I think I put on a convincing front.

"I'm *here*, Corbin, because *you're* here," he said. He slipped off his jacket and tossed it on the cushion he'd just vacated. "Anyway, right now, we both need some sleep. You'll obviously have to miss school tomorrow — we can get everything figured out then."

School. I didn't mention the suspension. Mike was right, the thing I most needed was sleep. Invisible weights sat heavy on my shoulders and my eyes stung from the fluorescent glare of the hospital lights and lack of rest.

I barely made it to my mattress before I was out.

Ten hours had disappeared by the time I opened my eyes again. For a second, maybe two, the world was normal. Then the awfulness of last night rushed in — blasts of sounds and sights and smells. Like Pop Rocks of horror exploding in my brain.

I got to my feet slowly, feeling like I might fall over if I made any sudden moves. Sounds beyond my room told me Mike was in the kitchen. I vaguely registered the fact that he was talking to someone … to Sitta, actually. I should have realized Sitta would have started squawking long before mid afternoon if he'd still been waiting for breakfast.

I made a quick stop in the bathroom and went to the kitchen doorway.

"Hey," Mike said. "This guy was warming up for a protest so I snuck him out of your room and got him some grub."

His thumb jerked toward the top of the fridge as he spoke, but Sitta had flown over his head and out into the hall. Probably shunning me over being fed by a stranger while I slept.

"Yeah, thanks," I said. I glanced uneasily at the frying pan sitting on the burner and the crumb-and-grease-covered plate near it on the counter. I wondered what he'd eaten and how long he planned to hang around here living on food I'd paid for.

"I called the hospital a while ago," Mike said. "Your mom had a good night and they're looking at moving her to Psych, either this evening or tomorrow morning if all goes well."

"She can't sign herself out, can she?"

"No — they've already had a judge sign off on keeping her there. For her own protection. And the doctor's orders are no visitors for the first week at least."

I tried to look disappointed about that, but if Mike was paying attention at all, he probably saw relief instead. A Mom-free week sounded like a holiday, as long as I knew she was safe and being taken care of.

"Why don't you grab some breakfast? I've got a few places to go, but I won't be long."

"I don't need a babysitter," I told him. "So, thanks and everything, but you really don't have to come back."

Mike took a minute to answer. When he did, all he said was, "I'll see you in a while."

"A while" was almost two hours and I'd started to think he'd changed his mind when I heard a key in the door.

"Where'd you get a key?" I asked as soon as he stepped inside. When I'd found him there earlier I'd assumed I'd left the place open, but apparently a locked door wouldn't have mattered.

"Your mom always makes sure I have a key to wherever you're living," he said. "In case of emergencies."

"Like last night, when she decided being a mother was too much bother?" I muttered.

"I don't think it's like that, Corbin," Mike said. He headed toward the kitchen and I noticed for the first time he was carrying three green bags full of stuff. Food, to be exact.

I followed, more interested in what was in the bags than what excuses he might make for my mother. He sat it all on the counter and nodded toward the bag nearest to me, signaling me to help unpack, which I was only too glad to do.

My bag had bananas, apples, carrots, onions, coffee cream, and a couple of big bags of potato chips. One plain and one barbecue. It took some self-control not to yank one open and stuff a handful in my mouth. I couldn't remember the last time I had chips.

Mike was finishing unpacking the other two bags and I saw, among a bunch of other stuff, that he'd bought hamburger and a package of buns.

"I was thinking burgers for supper," he said. "You ready to eat soon?"

"Yeah, sure," I said, as casually as I could. "I'll wash the frying pan."

Twenty-three minutes later I was sinking my teeth into a greasy, still-sizzling burger with cheese and ketchup and a thin slice of raw onion. I fought the urge to wolf it down, which was good because eating slower let me enjoy every amazing bite.

I wiped my chin with my sleeve when I was done and

found Mike watching me, grinning with a bit of meat stuck in his teeth.

"Want another one?" he said.

I let him talk me into it.

Twenty

"Okay, so let's talk."

I didn't want to talk. I wanted to lean back and enjoy the fact that I was too full to budge. When I could move again, I planned to take care of the sprouts I was growing for Sitta and go tell Taylor I was totally available to babysit for the next few weeks.

"Corbin?"

"Yeah, sorry." I forced my eyes open and looked across the room to where Mike sat. He had a piece of wood in his hands and was scraping at it with one of his whittling knives.

"First of all, you want to talk about what happened last night?"

"Not really."

"It must have been scary."

"I guess."

"You've been living this way for a long time."

"I don't remember things ever being different," I

admitted. "Mom keeps promising it's going to change, but it never does."

Mike didn't say anything to that. Maybe he thought he should be loyal. After all, Mom is his friend. Or maybe he knew there was nothing he *could* say.

"Is your dad still working in Barrow?"

"No, he finished his research in Alaska months ago," I said quietly. I knew that from his last letter, which I'd torn up as soon as I'd read it. "Now he's on some remote Norwegian island."

"Still off the grid quite a bit, then?"

"And halfway around the world," I said.

"In any case," Mike said, "he does the right thing in some ways. Like financially."

I shrugged. A "who cares" shrug. My father claims he thinks of me a lot and hopes to spend some time with me soon. But mostly, his letters and emails are about the places and people he encounters on jobs that guarantee he'll see me, at most, for a few weeks a year.

"I get why paying support isn't enough," Mike told me. "But without it you'd be on the verge of eviction right now, and there are enough problems to deal with without that."

"We're not getting evicted?"

"Nope. His support payment, and also her child

benefit, went into your mother's account after she crashed, so none of it was spent."

"How do you know what's in my mom's account?" I wasn't sure whether I felt uneasy or relieved that Mike apparently had access to our apartment and my mother's personal information.

"She gave me her info for online banking," he said. "That was a long time ago, in case it was ever needed. And there's a power of attorney too."

"So, the rent money's there?"

"Yep. And enough to cover a few other things. I feel it's only fair for you to know what's taking place, so I'm going to fill you in on everything, okay?"

When I nodded he went on. "I saw a social worker today — he looked into the file and they've approved me as a provisional foster parent for you. They'll even provide some funds toward your care. So, don't worry about anything."

Sitta picked that moment to swoop into the room — like a wingman that could actually fly. His timing was perfect, drawing Mike's attention away before he saw how his words had gotten to me. And then Mike was talking again and the danger was past.

"My boss let me have a couple of days off to get things sorted here, but I've got to be back at work on

Friday. Only thing, my shift starts at 7:00 in the morning. So, you'll have to get yourself to school. Can I rely on you for that?"

I laughed. There I'd been all choked up a few seconds ago and now I was like some giddy, over-emotional goofball. Mike raised an eyebrow, but didn't comment.

"I always get myself to school," I told him. "But actually, about that —"

I filled him in about the incident last week and the suspension. He asked to see the letter from the school and didn't look too happy as he read it.

"I'll come to the meeting, but this kind of thing can't be happening," he said. "Do you get in a lot of trouble?"

"Never," I said. "I mean, this is the first time. But don't worry, I won't mess up."

Except, I almost did, the very next morning.

Mike and I got to the school a few minutes before the meeting was supposed to start. The office worker had us sit in the waiting area, which was fine except when we were ushered into the conference room where the VP and guidance counselor were seated, I saw that Mack and his parents were there too.

Mack slid me a triumphant smirk — a twitch at the corner of his mouth, a mocking glint in his eyes. I didn't react.

The vice principal, Mr. Fanjoy, leaned forward, his elbows on the long, reddish table, and touched his fingertips together.

"We all know why we're here this morning," he said, sounding like he'd said the exact same thing the exact same way a thousand times before. "We hope to resolve this matter so that this young man," he paused to nod at Mack, "can feel safe, which he has every right to do."

Mack smirked again.

That was when I was close to saying or doing something that would have made the situation much, much worse. And the VP's next comments didn't do anything to calm me.

"Moreover," Fanjoy continued. "We hope to impress upon *you*, Corbin, that bullying is not, and *will* not, be tolerated in the halls of Middling Academy."

I saw, through my growing fury, that Mack's father was staring at me, the way you do when you're trying to intimidate someone. His mom, on the other hand, seemed to be carefully avoiding so much as a glance in my direction.

"Does Corbin have a history of bullying behaviors?" Mike asked suddenly.

"No, and we're hoping to keep it that way," said VP Fanjoy.

"It really seems out of character for him," Mike said mildly. "I can't help but think something precipitated his actions. Not to excuse what he did, but it does make me wonder. Would the other boy, perhaps, have any incidents of aggression on *his* record?"

"We obviously can't disclose another student's information," Fanjoy said. He looked just a little less sure of his control of the meeting.

I noticed that my heart rate, which had begun to race, was slowing again, and that I was feeling a whole lot calmer.

"Anyway, I believe an apology is required here," Fanjoy said. "And I must warn you, Corbin, that any further incidents of this nature will not be so easily resolved."

I got to my feet and took a step toward Mack. He shrunk back, although I don't know if that was an act or if he was genuinely afraid. You'd think it would be satisfying to think he might be scared of me, but the truth is, it bothered me a little.

"Mack," I said, "I'm sorry, man. I *never* do punk stuff like that. Actually, I think I might have had a fever or something that day — but, like I said, that's not who I am. It won't happen again."

I stuck my hand out and offered a friendly smile.

Mack glanced back and forth at his folks, who both nodded encouragingly. He reached his hand forward hesitantly and I shook it good and firm.

And I was back in class.

Twenty-one

W e were finishing an amazing supper of chicken fajitas one day, when Mike mentioned we'd be grabbing takeout on the way to the hospital the next afternoon.

"I imagine your mom will be glad to finally have a visitor," he added, picking a piece of lettuce off his shirt and popping it into his mouth.

"I thought she couldn't have anyone for a week," I said, taking my plate to the sink. Even as I said it, I realized it *had* been a week, which hardly seemed possible.

"Oh," I said.

"The days go by pretty quick when you're busy, huh?" Mike said.

Apparently. And there really *had* been a lot going on. I'd babysat Molly for Taylor on Thursday and again on Friday. That was when I finally met their mother, who told me right away to call her Sandra. She came home from her job as a dental technician a bit early, walking in on me lying on the floor performing a skit with some stuffed toys. Molly was giggling and clapping. Sandra paid me herself that day and gave me a few extra bucks. (Money I didn't have to spend on food. It's amazing to be able to save what I earn, at least for now.)

"It's great to have someone reliable to help with some of the babysitting," she said. "Taylor really deserves a break. Some weeks, when her dad's on the road — he's a long haul trucker, I don't know if Taylor mentioned that to you or not — but anyway, it's been a lot for her, especially the evenings I'm taking my courses."

"Courses?" I said.

"I know, I know. I already have a career, right? And it's not that it isn't satisfying, to some extent, but for a while now I've wanted to do more. So I finally took the plunge and signed up to get my counseling degree."

That sent a red flag up instantly. As nice as Sandra was, I made an excuse and got out of there quick. The last thing I needed was someone analyzing me!

Mike wasn't in the apartment when I got home a few minutes later, and it was weird how glad I was to hear his key in the lock shortly afterward.

Saturday, Mike announced we were going shopping and the two of us piled into his pickup and headed out. I assumed we were getting groceries, so it was a shock when we pulled up at a place where they sell used furniture.

There were huge rooms full of stuff in there, and I couldn't believe how cheap some of it was. Mike made the final decisions on what we got, but he asked my opinion and went with a couple of the things I liked. We came home with a futon and beanbag chair for the living room and a table with four chairs for the kitchen. The table is small, which is just right for now, but it also has a leaf to make it bigger.

The next day we got invited to eat at his folks' house. Well, his place too, I guess, since he rents a basement apartment there. We had roast chicken with stuffing and gravy and potatoes and peas and a while later his mom served warm cherry pie and ice cream. And it wasn't even a special occasion.

Then when we left, Mike said he had to grab something from his place, and when he came back he was lugging a blanket-covered smart TV.

"There's no cable or anything at the apartment," I told him.

"There will be tomorrow," he said with a grin.

I've been trying to relax and enjoy all these changes and not worry about later. Besides, I can't help feeling optimistic — as though the worst stuff is over with and things are going to be better from now on.

As crazy as it sounds, I have this theory that Sitta brought good luck with him. Not just by being there for company, either. I keep remembering how he said, "Spell. Spell," the night Mom went into the hospital. And yeah, that was a bad night, but so much turned around since then. It really feels like something magic, something good and lasting is happening.

Speaking of Sitta, Izelle was impressed — way more than the modest furnishings deserved, to be honest — when she came for her Monday visit with him.

"Look at this place!" she said. "This is great! What changed your mom's mind — you know, about the carbon footprint and everything?"

"Actually, she's sick again and a friend of hers is staying here," I explained. "He thought it would be nice to have something to sit on."

"Sitta likes it too," I added, although that was mainly made up. Sitta hadn't expressed an opinion one way or the other.

Izelle's eyes lit up at that and she launched into one of her non-stop talking jags. I kind of like when she does that because it requires so little in return. An occasional grunt, nod, or murmur and she's good.

She chattered away, jumping from subject to subject like a linguistic gymnast. As usual, she accompanied herself with hand gestures, graceful little sweeping motions one second and vicious air stabs the next.

And while I was watching and half listening to her, it occurred to me that Izelle has become a friend.

It's been a while since I had a friend. A real one anyway. It's strange, how she snuck into that spot without me even knowing it was happening.

As I was thinking this, her words trailed off and she gave me a curious look.

"What?" she said.

I blinked at the question and said, "Huh?"

"You're looking at me weird."

And I don't know why, exactly. Maybe all the good things that had been happening came together in a way that made me feel invincible at that moment, or maybe I saw how unfair it would be to her if it all fell apart and I just disappeared with Sitta one day, but something shifted inside me.

I started talking. I told her everything. The truth about my mother, about how we lived, how often we moved — the words just kept coming and coming. When I finally stopped, she had everything she needed to reclaim Sitta, turn her back, and treat me like the liar I'd been.

"You should have told me the truth," she said after the silence in the room had stretched itself tight.

"I know. I'm sorry."

"You should be," she said, nodding. "I mean, I get why you lied, but —"

"Look, if you want Sitta back —" I said. That was as far as I got.

Izelle's eyes flashed with anger.

"*What*?" she said. "That's not what I meant! Besides, I'm glad Sitta's with you; I can see how good that must be — for both of you. But I could have been a better friend if I'd known. I wouldn't have been mad, or given you a hard time when you kept me away. And I might have been able to help more with food for Sitta."

That conversation kept sinking in over the next few days. It left a lingering good feeling in me that lasted right up until the first visit with Mom.

The hallway to the Psych Unit was painted a pale green, which someone once told me is a calming color. It doesn't seem to be having much of an impact on the patients there, judging by the laments and protests we heard.

Mom wasn't contributing to the noise. She was in her room, sitting in the visitor chair in the corner, staring out the window. Mike nudged me forward at the doorway. I stepped inside and took a few tentative steps toward her.

"Hi, Mom," I said.

Her head turned slowly and her eyes rested on me without any sign of enthusiasm. But at least she answered.

"Hi, Corbin."

"How are you feeling?" I asked. I took another, very small step toward her.

"Well, they've got me trapped like an animal, in here with a bunch of crazies," she said. "So how do you think I am?"

"Rhea," Mike said, stepping into the room, "sorry we haven't been in before. We came as soon as the doctor said you were up for visitors."

Mom's gaze drifted to Mike and hovered on him in a kind of puzzled way, like she either wasn't sure who he was or couldn't figure out why he was there.

"Mike's been staying at our place while you're ... away," I said.

"Okay," she said. And that was the last word she uttered while we were there. Her face swiveled back to the window and although Mike and I made a few more attempts to talk, she either couldn't or wouldn't say anything else.

"Okay then," Mike said at last. "We just wanted

to drop by and say hello and see how you were doing. We'll be back in a couple of days — is there anything you'd like us to bring you?"

Silence.

Mike waited for a couple of minutes and when it was obvious he wouldn't be getting an answer, he gave me a nod.

"Bye, Mom," I said, trying not to sound glad to be leaving.

We stopped at the nurses' station before heading out into the night, but there wasn't much new they could tell us. Dr. Scaria was seeing Mom every day and they were trying her on some new meds. Hopefully, they told us, there'd be some improvement soon.

None of that is new, or unusual. What *is* new is this time I suddenly believe improvement is possible. Because things have been changing.

They definitely have.

Twenty-two

I used to hate the sound of a knock at the door. Until we moved here, a knock generally meant someone angry was going to be in the hallway outside our apartment.

It still makes me a bit jumpy, but only for a second. Only as long as it takes to remind myself that we're not getting kicked out of here and no one's coming to confront Mom about something she said or did.

Today's knock found me a bit jittery, though, but that was only because this is the first time I've ever invited a guest for dinner. I'd asked Mike if it was okay and he was all for it.

"Heck, yeah. I could definitely stand having some-one to look at besides you," he said. But he laughed to show me he wasn't serious.

I'd given the place a quick inspection to make sure it looked okay a few minutes ago, although that hasn't been much of an issue since Mike's been staying here. With Mom, the place was either spotless or at the mercy of whatever I happened to do. That wasn't usually too much aside from washing the dishes when the pile got too high.

Mike's approach is organized, but surprisingly easy. The plan he put in place started when he'd been here a couple of days and happened to walk into my room to ask me something.

"Dude, your room stinks," he said. "Is that the bird cage or what?"

That wasn't it. I'd been careful about cleaning the cage because one of the articles I'd read said that was important for keeping your parakeet healthy.

Mike started sniffing around — literally — and discovered the smell was coming from the clothes in my closet.

"Okay, so this stuff is rank," he said. "When's the last time you did laundry?"

I couldn't remember, but it had been a while. I'd washed a few things out in the bathroom sink, but for the most part I'd kept rotating the rest. Clean clothes hadn't been a priority when the bit of money I made was needed for food.

The next thing I knew, Mike had made a quick trip to the store for laundry soap and change, and the washers downstairs were full of my stuff.

After that he made a schedule for doing laundry and other things like sweeping and mopping the floors, doing dishes, and cleaning the bathroom. We take turns at everything and none of it ever takes long. What I like about it is the place never feels embarrassing.

Even so, I did a quick check today, and also made sure the table was set right, with the fork on the left like Mom taught me during one of her good periods.

"Just remember," she'd told me, "'fork' and 'left' both have four letters, while 'knife,' 'spoon,' and 'right' all have five. Just keep them matched and you'll never get the silverware wrong."

That memory made me feel sad. Why couldn't she have leveled out and stayed that way? Sometimes it felt as if the bad days — so many bad days — had wiped out all the good ones.

"You getting the door?" Mike asked from the kitchen, where he was stirring sauce.

I jerked my brain back to the present and hurried to the door, pulling it open and smiling at our guest.

"Come on in," I said.

Mr. Zinbendal had dressed up! I couldn't help smiling as he made his way into the living room wearing dark gray pants, a light blue shirt, and red suspenders. Mike came around the corner just as our neighbor reached the futon. I introduced them and they shook hands.

"This is quite a treat," Mr. Zinbendal told me, beaming. "I sure appreciate the invitation."

"Well, we hope you like spaghetti," I said.

"One of my favorites!" he answered. "And it smells scrumptious."

"We're nearly ready to start," Mike said. "The pasta just needs another minute or two. We might as well get ourselves situated at the table."

Half an hour later we were all stuffed full. Mike had made garlic bread to go with the spaghetti, which was delicious too. It was my night for dishes, but Mike offered to switch.

"You go on ahead and visit with your guest in the other room while I make coffee and put out some cookies."

Sitting there, talking with "my guest" felt good. Mr. Zinbendal told me about some of the jobs he'd had when he was young.

"I started out as a gas station attendant," he said. "Nobody pumped their own gas back then. We cleaned the windshields and checked the oil too; those were free services. Lots of folks would ask for five dollars, or sometimes even two dollars worth of gas, and that would get them around for days.

"Later, I got work cleaning and operating printing presses. That was a night job, but I didn't mind it. My eyes were a good deal better back then, which was important because the machinery had a lot of delicate parts that had to be handled carefully."

He shifted to the side a little, getting more comfortable, and noticed Mike's latest whittling project, perched on a stack of books. It was too soon to say what it was supposed to be. Mr. Zinbendal reached over and picked it up, examining all sides of it.

"Lost art, whittling," he said after a moment. "I don't suppose this is yours?"

"No, Mike does them," I said quickly. "He told me his grandfather used to whittle all kinds of things."

Mike had told me he'd taken it up to make his grandfather proud. I didn't see much to be proud of in the crude figures he produced, but I kept that opinion to myself.

Mike appeared just then with Mr. Zinbendal's coffee and a plate of Oreos. He had a mug for me too, but it was full of milk. Not that I minded, since milk is perfect with cookies.

"You know," Mr. Zinbendal said, halfway through his second cookie, "I owe you an apology."

"What for?" I asked, surprised.

"When you first moved in, I must have seemed downright un-neighborly," he said. "But the thing was, I hadn't seen my daughter in a long while, and just around that time I'd written to her, asking her to come and pick out whatever she wanted from her mother's china collection. Every time I heard footsteps getting to the end of the hall, I couldn't help checking to see if it was her."

I thought about how he'd seemed cranky and nosy back then. What I'd actually been seeing was sadness and disappointment.

"Did she ever come over?" I asked.

He shook his head. His face was sad. "We had a falling out, almost four years ago. But that was no reason for me to be unfriendly toward my new neighbors."

"It's okay," I said. "And anyway, we're friends now."

After he'd gone across the hall, back to his own apartment, and I'd finished my homework, I had a talk with Sitta.

"See, Sitta. You never know what someone else is going through. It's really easy to forget that other people have problems too."

"Paw! Paw!" Sitta said. "Cool paw!"

"I wish I could help the poor old guy," I said as I

slipped Sitta into his cage and fastened the door shut. "Any ideas?"

But Sitta was busy at his water dish and had nothing else to say.

Twenty-three

"Do you want some time to talk with your mom alone today?"

Mike's question didn't surprise me. He's asked it almost every time we've visited the hospital for the last few weeks. I'd always said I didn't want to. But now, I felt like it was time.

"Yeah, I guess so."

"I'll be in the patient lounge then. Just come get me whenever you want."

"Okay. Thanks."

My feet didn't seem to be in any kind of rush to get to her room, even though she'd been slowly improving. I saw more signs of that with each visit and whether it was a new drug or a new combination of drugs, she'd evened out a lot.

She wasn't there when I first went in, but I doubted I'd find her in the lounge. For someone who's directed traffic at a busy intersection, dragged her kid up and down the city streets in the middle of the night, and done all kinds of other bizarre things, Mom sees herself as "normal" compared to the other patients. She doesn't like to associate with them.

"Well, hello there."

I turned to find her in the doorway, holding a cup of water in one hand and a plastic jug in the other. Both were full of water and crushed ice — like flavorless slushies.

"Hi, Mom."

"The air in here is so dry — it's a challenge to stay hydrated," she said before lifting the cup to her lips and taking a long drink. She refilled it from the jug before plunking herself on the side of the bed and setting the jug on her tray. "You just get here?"

"Yes," I said. Then, remembering the routine, I asked, "How are you feeling these days, Mom?"

"Bored," she answered. "There's not much to do in here. I know you guys brought me some stuff to read, but it's hard to concentrate. I need to get out of this place."

"Do you know when?" I asked. "You're getting out, I mean?"

"Who knows. They play with people's lives like we're just here for their amusement," she said with a shrug.

"You're better, though, right? So it probably won't be too long."

"I hope not kiddo. I can't wait for things to get back to normal."

Every moment of my life before now, I would have said nothing to that. I would have let it slide past or — more likely, actually — even agreed with her. This moment was different.

"You can't really call the way we live normal, though, can you?" I said.

Mom's head lifted slowly. Her mouth twitched and her eyes narrowed. I braced myself, fighting the urge to pretend my words had been some kind of joke.

"Meaning what?" she said.

"Meaning things are okay for a while, but then it gets crazy —"

The second the word "crazy" left my mouth I wished I could haul it back in, swallow it, erase it from the air.

"*What* did you say?" Mom asked. A faint blush of pink was creeping over her face.

"I just meant that *things* get … weird sometimes. I wasn't talking about *you*."

"Oh, *no*?" Even with the dulling effect of her meds, Mom's words were dipped in frost and fury. "So, if it's not me, what causes all this *craziness*? And *weirdness*?"

"Forget it," I said. Once again, I'd lost my nerve. I told myself at least I'd made a start at telling her how I felt. Honestly, I don't know why I even tried. You can't win an argument with my mother. Not that I'd been aiming for an argument.

"I will *not* forget it," she told me. "How dare you come in here and start accusing me of things? Why do you think I'm even in here? Because I'm exhausted, that's why! Because everything falls on *my* shoulders. And instead of letting me rest, and recover, you attack me!"

"You are *not* here because you're exhausted," I said, trying to stay calm. "You're here because you tried to *kill yourself.*"

In a flash, Mom's arm drew back and the cup she'd been holding came flying at me. I ducked, but still got hit by the ice and water cascading out as it whipped past me.

"I hate you," I hissed. I know I meant it, for those few seconds. But the guilt and shame of the words stabbed through the hardness my heart needed for them to be true. And then they were a lie.

Mom's face crumbled and, oddly enough, she reached toward me for comfort, her hands fluttering and beckoning. I grabbed onto her and told her I was sorry and I hadn't meant it and I loved her and everything was going to be okay. I said it all, over and over while she sobbed like she might never stop.

On the way home with Mike later I wondered why I'd even tried to talk to Mom about how things are. I know she can't help what her illness does to her. What she *could* help — like staying on her meds even if they make her feel like a stranger in her own body, as she's told me more than once when she's "adjusting" the dosage against doctor's orders — she decides she *can't*.

Having Mike around has been great. I'd even tell him so, except I bet he'd be embarrassed.

Besides, I keep reminding myself, this is temporary, just like I overheard him telling someone on the phone the other day.

I'd come back from babysitting Molly while he was in the kitchen, and he didn't realize I was there.

"I don't know. Maybe another week or two," he'd been saying. "I really can't make plans until Rhea gets home."

My heart sank. Not because I ever thought Mike was going to be here long term, but it made Mom's return seem so close.

Just when I was getting used to normal.

Twenty-four

I can cook some pretty cool meals now, as long as I have the stuff that goes into them.

Some are way easier than you'd think. Butter chicken and rice, for example, which is awesome even with sauce from a jar. Or stew, which I used to find boring. Mike showed me how to season it so there's lots of flavor. The secret is making sure it's got the right herbs and stuff, depending on what kind you're making. Tacos are super simple too, and there are probably half a dozen other meals I can make.

I've been discovering a lot, with Mike here. Like how good it feels to always have a clean place and clean clothes, how much better I do in school when I eat right and get enough rest, and how much I seriously hate living with the chaos my mother's illness can cause.

It was all upbeat until that last part, right? What am I supposed to say? After a month of not having to worry about, well, *anything* really, the thought of going back to that roller-coaster way of life again makes my stomach queasy.

Not that it matters. Mike broke it to me a while ago that she's coming home tomorrow morning.

"I'd like to be here to help her get settled back in," he said, "but I couldn't get the day off."

"Should I stay home from school?" I asked.

"Definitely not. You don't want to be missing school unless you have to," he said.

That was fine with me.

"I'll be over after work," he reassured me. "I left Rhea a note that I'm going to pick up takeout and have supper here. Then I'll be out of your hair."

"It hasn't been *that* bad," I told him.

He laughed. "I agree," he said.

Then he got serious.

"Anything you want to talk about?" he asked. A familiar question.

I knew what he was asking, but I really had nothing to say. How could I, when I never know what I need to be ready for next?

On my walk home from school the next day I found myself getting angry.

If you've never felt your stomach twisting in knots, wondering what you'd find at home after a day at school, you probably can't imagine the incredible relief there'd been in not having that worry for the past four weeks.

I guess it would be just as hard to understand the anxiety that gripped me on my way up the stairs to my apartment, knowing my mother was back.

The last couple of visits with Mom at the hospital had been okay. So that was good. Not so good was the fact that the talks I'd hoped for hadn't happened. She just got angry when I didn't go along with her, pretending everything was fine. Which meant none of the things bothering me got discussed. Not with Mom anyway.

I *did* talk to Sitta.

"No pressure, buddy, but if you have any secret powers, don't be shy to use them."

Sitta's response was a tilted head followed by a bit of preening. I told myself I wasn't disappointed. I hadn't really expected him to do anything. Or, if I had, it was in a small and not-at-all serious way.

Because of course I know he didn't *actually* do anything the night he said, "Spell, spell!" I'm not superstitious enough to think it was anything more than a coincidence — the way everything changed dramatically right after that.

As I stood in the hallway outside our apartment, I wondered what I might have to deal with inside. It shouldn't be anything — not yet. Not this soon after the last spiral.

The pattern rarely varies. Mom is a bit like a balloon — floating along peacefully for a while and then, as if someone stuck a pin into her, flying around like mad until she lands face down on the floor, limp and deflated.

I took a deep breath, stuck my key in the lock, and turned the doorknob.

"Corbin? Is that you, hon?" Mom's voice greeted me before her smile. She emerged from the kitchen and hurried toward me.

"Hi, Mom." A grin showed up on my face. She looked happy. And pretty.

"I was going to cook a nice dinner for you," she said as she reached out for a hug. "But Mike's bringing something. Chicken, I hope."

"I hope so too," I agreed.

"The place looks great," she said. "You guys took good care of things."

"Mike made a schedule," I told her.

"Sounds like a good idea," she said. "Maybe we should make one too."

I almost suggested using Mike's. Almost. What stopped me was the sudden realization that Mom's eyes weren't smiling. It stopped at her mouth. That told me she was trying to look and feel a whole lot happier than she actually did. It also meant it would be a bad idea to contradict anything she said. Even something simple could upset whatever thin grip she had on her forced good cheer.

"Sure!" I agreed. Because when Mom's trying so hard, I try right along with her. A couple of pretenders, but sometimes it feels pretty close to real.

I took care of Sitta and then Mom and I went to the kitchen and sat at the table. Mom made herself a cup of tea and I poured a glass of milk. I knew she'd have questions. She always does when she's been absent, even if her absence hasn't actually taken her out of wherever we're living. It's like she needs to fill in the gap. She admitted once that she feels guilty for missing chunks of my life.

Sure enough, she started asking me things.

— How was school going? (Fine. Good, really.)
— Did the girl I got Sitta from — what was her name again — still come over? (Her name's Izelle and yes, she comes to visit Sitta on Mondays. He likes it when she comes to see him.)
— Was I enjoying having the bird? (A lot. And I've

learned some cool things about taking care of a bird, like sprouting things for him and stuff.)

When she asked me if there was anything new going on with me, I knew that would be the last question. I told her about the babysitting job with Molly, even though it wasn't exactly new, because I hadn't told her about it before.

"Well," Mom said, "I guess we're all caught up now."

She reached over and patted my hand. A tell. I waited for what I knew was coming next.

"Corbin, I know things have been hard on you lately."

"I'm okay," I told her.

"That's not the point. You shouldn't have to be worrying about me, and I know you do. Because of the illness."

I said nothing to that. My throat gets tight at this part of our catch-up talk.

"I just want you to know that things are going to be different from now on."

Sure they are. No. Try to be optimistic. This could be the time!

"I promise."

Promise number — I've lost track. Forty, maybe?

Again I tell myself to stop. Turn off the cynicism. But I couldn't quite find the valve as she continued.

She spent a good half hour trying to persuade me to believe her. Not that I said I didn't, but if you've broken your word as many times as Mom has, you probably know you've really got to sell it.

And the thin thread of hope I've been clutching for so long told me one more time that it's possible. It's always possible. This time could be different.

Mike got there just after I'd finished doing my homework.

He brought Thai food. Mom told him it was exactly what she'd been hoping for.

Twenty-five

Mom has been back at home for nearly two months and so far she's doing pretty well. That used to be practically the only thing that mattered in my world, because so much depended on it. But lately I've realized something else that's important. To me.

I want to stay here, in our apartment on Westlester Street, until I graduate.

Before we moved here, the longest we'd ever lived in one place was when we had an apartment on Standing Crescent. The landlord there was nice. He rode out a couple of Mom's episodes and even let her work off a delinquent month's rent by having her clean the hallways for a while.

That was a few years ago, and we lived there for nine months. I didn't like it though. The apartment was dark and musty and there always seemed to be a lot of noise in the hallways.

There was a homeless man who often sat near our

building there, and I used to watch the way people hurried past, acting as if they didn't even see him. In a strange way I felt like we were kind of the same, because there were times when I needed help and no one saw how scared or desperate I was.

I wished I could do something for the homeless man, but of course I had no money and it seemed I had nothing to offer him. Except, I discovered that wasn't quite true. I did have something.

For the rest of the time we lived there, I stopped and talked to him whenever I was going by. Not about anything important. Just, "Hi, how are you?" kind of stuff.

His name was Carl.

Talking to Carl didn't put food in his stomach, or warm socks on his feet, but I saw, after a while, that it gave him something else. Exactly what, I'm not sure, but whatever it was, it made him smile.

After we moved, I realized that the whole time we lived there, Carl was the only one who got to know my name or asked me how I was doing.

I didn't miss the place when the landlord finally ran out of patience, but I kind of missed Carl. I still think about him now and then and I hope he's okay.

The apartment we're in now is different than any-where else I can remember living. It's the first one that's felt like home. Like there's a community we belong to.

Mr. Zinbendal is nothing like he seemed at first. I like him a lot, especially the cool stories he tells about the old days. He plays cribbage with me and pretends he's trying to cheat, but I know he isn't really because he always makes sure I catch him. It makes both of us laugh.

He's become friends with Mom too, although some-times I see him looking at her sadly and I know he's thinking about his own daughter. A month after Mom got out of the hospital he gave us a recliner he had in his storage unit. It used to be his wife's favorite chair and he never could bring himself to sit in it after she had a stroke and died. It's really comfortable, and it makes him happy to see us using it.

Most weeks we take turns having meals at each others' places. Mom says Mr. Zinbendal reminds her a little of her grandfather and he says we've become like family.

And there's Taylor and Molly and their mom, Sandra. I met their dad once too, but a long haul trucker isn't home that much. Molly runs and hugs me when I go there to babysit. She calls me Co-bin and she trusts me for things like making sure her food isn't too hot, or catching her when she flings herself off the couch.

And there's Izelle, who I count even though she doesn't live in the building. She still comes to see Sitta every week, but we also hang out sometimes. Ever since I told her the truth about my mom she keeps proving I was right to be honest with her. For one thing, she didn't start acting all different, and — more important — she didn't blab it around school. Not a word. That made it easy to tell her other stuff I've never talked about before — to anyone. Of course, she can't fix my problems or anything like that, but just having someone to talk to makes a big difference. It sort of makes me feel, I don't know, lighter, in a way.

Then there's Mom.

Mom got a job not long after her last hospital stay, at a dry-cleaning place called *So Fresh Cleaners*. She works the counter, waiting on the customers when they bring garments in or pick them up. It's a twenty-minute bus ride each way and her shift starts at 8:00 every morning, which means I have the apartment to myself before school.

Every weekend we go grocery shopping and Mom lets me help pick things out, since I do a lot of the cooking. Sometimes Mike takes us and we all have lunch out somewhere, but if he's busy, Mom and I manage okay on the bus.

One day, as we were putting away our grub, Mom noticed a can of black olives in the cupboard.

"When did we get these?" she asked, wrinkling her nose. Mom isn't a fan of olives.

"Mike got them when he was staying here," I said.

Mom put the can back. She was silent for a few seconds and then, without warning, she reached over and gave me a fierce hug.

"I'm sorry things get so hard sometimes," she said. "I hope you know, in spite of all that, how much — how *very* much I love you."

"I know, Mom," I said. I hugged her back.

"You're the only thing," she said, leaning away enough to look me in the eyes, "the *only* thing that really, truly matters to me."

She let go then and put the olives back in the cupboard.

"That's why I made those arrangements with Mike," she said quietly, "even though I hated the idea of someone else here in my place."

"Everything's okay now, though," I said. "Better than okay." And it was true.

Evenings are good too. Mom goes to bed early most nights — she gets tired easily, but I'm not sure if it's just that. Mike gave us a sweet deal on the television he brought here (an excuse to get a bigger one for his place he said) so it's ours now, but Mom doesn't seem to enjoy watching it. She keeps complaining that it's hard to follow what's happening because the story lines jump around too much. Except, I can tell she's not really paying attention most of the time, which is probably because of the meds she's on. Her doctor always tells her to be patient and wait out the side effects.

That doesn't really bother me since I like watching TV alone anyway.

So, yeah. Things have been decent. Which is what got me thinking about how much I want it to stay that way. And how great it would be to stay here.

It took me a while to bring that up with Mom. That had to be handled just right, by which I mean approached casually. Otherwise, Mom might have felt I was making accusations and gotten defensive. This time, I just worked it into the conversation.

It was Sunday afternoon. We'd gone to church that morning (something we do once in a while when Mom gets the urge) and walked home after the service was over.

On the way, we stopped at a place where they sell pizza by the slice. Mom got pepperoni and I got one

Hawaiian and one deluxe. Just up the road from there was a tiny park — the kind with a tree, a couple of bushes, a patch of grass, and a bench. We sat there to eat — Mom taking nibble-sized bites of her slice while I wolfed mine down. She was only halfway through hers when I'd finished.

"This is a nice spot," I observed, looking around. "You couldn't tell it was here when it was still snowy."

"Not very private, though," Mom said.

"True. But I like this neighborhood. I'm glad we moved here."

"Mmm," said Mom.

"I like our building too."

Mom stopped eating and looked at me. "What do you like about it?"

"The people, I guess. They're nicer than other places we've lived."

Mom seemed to consider that. She's not dumb, so she had to know the difference had more to do with how things were going in our lives. I mean, you can find nice people and not so nice people pretty much anywhere.

"We *do* have a good neighbor," she said after a bit.

"Do you think we can stay here?"

"That's something you want?" she said slowly.

"Yes."

"It's pretty hard to make permanent plans," Mom told me.

"Not permanent, exactly. But could we stay until I finish high school?"

Mom bit into her pizza again. She chewed and swallowed before answering.

"We have to live somewhere," she said. "Might as well be where we are now, if you like it so much."

"Thanks, Mom," I said. I could hardly believe how well the conversation had gone. I wasn't sure I should press my luck, but I couldn't help it. Just a little. I did something that Mom used to do with me a lot when I was younger.

"Care to do a pinkie swear?" I said, leaning in and speaking in a whisper the way she always had.

Mom's eyes lit up with laughter. She held up her right hand and circled my little finger with hers.

"You've got it," she said. "I swear!"

It was the most hopeful I could ever remember feeling.

Twenty-six

"I told you Sitta was brilliant! Just look at him!"

Sitta *is* smart, don't get me wrong, but I had to hide a smile at the boast Izelle had just made. I turned to her.

"What did he do?" I asked, even though I'd been watching too.

"Molly tried to sneak up on him — didn't you see it? Sitta kept moving just out of her reach until he reached the corner, then he flew back to where he started."

"Molly's pretty scary sometimes," I said.

Izelle laughed. "To you maybe. I think she's as cute as a button."

"I haven't seen a lot of super cute buttons," I said, watching as Molly gave up her stealth approach and made a stubby-legged run at Sitta, who lifted into the air at the last second.

"See? He's a genius!" Izelle insisted.

"Even though the human he's outsmarting is still in diapers?" I asked. This got me a playful swat on the arm.

"Muffoo," said Molly. She'd abandoned the chase and had come to stand squarely in front of me.

"We don't have any muffins," I told her, "but I think I can find you a snack if Izelle will watch you while I go check."

"Sure." Izelle reached for the bag of toys Taylor had dropped off along with Molly about half an hour earlier.

It was the first time I'd ever babysat Molly at my place. Taylor had come to the door looking agitated only minutes after Izelle and I got there after school.

"Can you watch Molly for, maybe an hour or so?" she asked. Then, spying Izelle, "Oh. You have company. But I can bring her here if that's okay."

I'd agreed, although I didn't know what Izelle would think of a toddler running around while she was having her visit with Sitta. Molly can get pretty wild.

Izelle hadn't minded at all. The sound of the two of them singing *Itsy Bitsy Spider* reached me as I washed, cored, and sliced an apple. I put some little cheese cubes in the center of a plate and arranged the apple slices around it like flower petals, because Molly loves it when her food looks special.

"Oooh!" Izelle said when I took the snack to Molly. "Look, Molly! What's this?"

"Fower!" Molly said. She's not a big fan of the letter L yet.

"That's *right* ... flower!" Izelle said. She clapped so of course Molly and I joined in.

"FOWER!" Molly said again, much louder. Her eyes snapped and shone with excitement and pride.

There was a lot of clapping for the next few minutes as Molly repeated her big announcement, looking back and forth between me and Izelle. Eventually, she either got bored or hunger won out, and she wound down and gobbled the "fower" up.

Taylor was back in less than an hour. She smiled, but it was obviously forced and her eyes were angry.

"Thanks, Corbin," she said. "I'll take pea pod off your hands now."

Molly was already racing toward her, arms lifted and joy on her little face. Taylor scooped her up and planted a kiss on her chubby cheek. "Were you good for Corbin?" she asked.

"Of course she was," I said. "Hang on and I'll grab her stuff."

I did that, with Izelle's help, while Molly chattered away with her own private language. I can never figure out if she's actually trying to say something, or just mimicking conversation with random sounds.

When I passed Taylor the bag with Molly's things, she leaned in and said, "If DJ ever comes to my place when you're watching Molly, don't let him in."

"What did he do?" I blurted before I could stop myself.

"Nothing to her," Taylor said, quickly. "But I just broke up with the cheating lowlife and I don't want him around."

I had no clue what to say to that, but it didn't matter. She hoisted Molly up to her hip, said, "Thanks again," and was gone.

The door had barely closed behind Taylor and Molly when I saw that Izelle was getting ready to leave too. She'd coaxed Sitta to perch on her hand and was kissing his beak, which was her usual way of saying goodbye.

"I have to go," she said, turning to me. "My mom got a promotion at work and we're eating out somewhere fancy to celebrate."

"You can come again another day this week if you want," I said.

"Thanks!" she said. "I'm not sure if I can, but I'll let you know."

"Okay, well, see you tomorrow."

And she was gone. The apartment felt oddly quiet after having Izelle and Molly both there and I was considering asking Mr. Zinbendal if he wanted to have a game of crib, or his new favorite — Scrabble. Neither one of us is any good at it, but he loves to play anyway.

Then Mom came in.

"Hey, kiddo!" she said.

A flush of fear raced through me. I took a couple of deep breaths and told myself not to panic.

"You get off work early?" I said.

"Sure did. It was quiet and after the rough day I had they must have thought I deserved a break."

Relief. Nothing to worry about. People get off early all the time when there are slow days.

"What happened? I mean, what was the rough part?" I asked.

"Customers and their crazy demands," Mom said with a light laugh.

I didn't push it. Why look for trouble where there might be none?

I told myself that for a couple of days. Then I snuck into Mom's room when she wasn't home and I checked her meds. Or, more exactly, I counted them. And I made a note of how many she had of each type of pill, and how many she was supposed to be taking each day. Because trouble usually starts when she decides the dosages her doctor ordered aren't working. Then she'll play around with them, making whatever adjustments she thinks are a good idea.

It was the eleventh of the month. If I counted everything again in a week's time, it would be easy to see if she was taking them as prescribed or not.

Feeling guilty for being suspicious, for not giving Mom the benefit of the doubt, I hid the note I'd made under some old school stuff on the shelf in my closet. I promised myself I wasn't even going to think about it again until the week was up.

Twenty-seven

I held out for five days before I did another count.

By then, it didn't matter anyway. By then I knew what I was going to find. But, in fairness, before I go into that, I need to stop and remember why.

Why it kept happening.

Why Mom decided time after time that she knew more than the doctors.

"It's *my* body," I had often heard her say. "Who knows it better than I do?"

She used to boast about how clever she was whenever she started mucking around with her meds. She'd describe how much better she felt and how much clearer her thinking was. She insisted that things were making sense again. When I was younger, she made me into a strange sort of co-conspirator, a child cheering on his mother's bad choices and feeling the weight of their consequences later in an avalanche of guilt and confusion and fear.

She doesn't brag anymore. Now she hides and lies and denies. Most likely some part of her knows she's heading for trouble, but I guess she always finds a way to convince herself it's not going to happen again. That's probably not hard to do between the short period of time she thinks everything is going well — and when the edges of her world start to shift and slide.

I've heard her say she feels more alive and in control. More like herself. It's hard to blame her for wanting that, or for letting herself hope each time that it will all turn out okay. Except it never does and I can't understand why she still hasn't grasped that it never will.

There are always signs when trouble is coming and I've seen a few of those signs in the past five days, even though I was trying to stay cool and not worry. That turned out to be impossible. Things started to prickle and crawl on my skin, which is not something a person's brain can just ignore.

The first time that happened was last week, on the day she breezed through the door after being sent home early. And I guess I was playing a game of my own, trying to believe it might be totally innocent. She's been at that job for a couple of months and had never been sent home before her regular shift ended, although there had to have been lots of other times when the place wasn't busy.

There was also the way she'd mentioned it being a rough day with customers and their crazy demands. If I'd been hearing that from anyone else, there'd have been no reason to doubt it. But I was hearing from my mother.

One of the first giveaways Mom is headed for trouble is that she'll start finding fault with her job. And not just one thing — there will be one problem after another. That's definitely been happening.

It began with Mom's boss, Mrs. Ohanian. Mom had described her in the past as a nice woman, a bit demanding, but fair and someone who worked every bit as hard as her employees. The new version has turned Mrs. Ohanian into an incompetent who watches Mom like a hawk, complains for no reason, and is just generally horrid.

Other workplace complaints that appeared out of nowhere this week were: the place is drafty, the customers are impossible to please, and other workers are deliberately putting items in the wrong order just to confuse and embarrass her.

More alarming was the fact that Mom's mood was shifting at home. A sullen undercurrent of suspicion had slid into place and I often felt her watching me, looking for evidence of ... something. A sign of betrayal, maybe. A hint of rebellion.

But anyone can have a bad week, so even with all of that — and, honestly, because I didn't want to face it — I wouldn't let myself be sure of what it meant. Until today.

Today was the first time we'd invited both Mike and Mr. Zinbendal over for supper. I was in charge of the cooking and had decided to make chicken thighs with rice and Caesar salad. That would have sounded impressive to me before, but not since Mike showed me how easy a lot of meals are to prepare.

I sprinkled some mixed herbs over the chicken, put a bit of water in the pan, and stuck it in the oven. All it would need after that was a bit of basting. The rice came in an envelope with its own flavoring, the kind you dump into a pot with water and stir once in a while. And the salad was in a bag that included everything, so all I had to do was rinse the romaine and mix it all up just before we were ready to eat.

Mr. Zinbendal arrived first. He had a cellophane

package with six chocolate cupcakes in it. The kind with huge mounds of frosting on top.

"I brought dessert — in case you didn't have time to bake," he said with a chuckle.

"Thanks!" I told him. "These look great."

I've discovered that Mr. Zinbendal has quite a sweet tooth. His kitchen is never short on cakes and pies and pastries and when he's invited me and Mom for supper there were always at least two dessert choices after the meal.

We hardly ever have stuff like that at our place, so I suspected he brought the cupcakes to make sure there was a treat available after we ate. That was fine with me.

He asked me about school — the usual questions except he paid close attention to my answers so I didn't mind. And he had a funny talk with Sitta.

"You ever think about getting married, bird?" Mr. Zinbendal cocked his head to the side, mimicking Sitta's reaction. "Yes, it's true, you'd have to share your cage, but a wife can be good company."

Sitta flew down the hall.

"I see you're not convinced," Mr. Zinbendal called after him. "But maybe you just haven't met the right girl yet. You have to keep an open mind."

"He doesn't get a lot of chances to meet other birds," I pointed out.

Mr. Zinbendal smiled.

"When it's meant to be, it will happen," he said. Then, "Something smells awfully good."

"Chicken," I said. I was going to tell him more, but a knock at the door drew me away.

"You have a key," I said, opening it to Mike. "Plus, it wasn't even locked."

He gave me a one-armed sort-of hug before answering.

"I'm still not going to walk in anytime I like."

"Not even when you're invited?"

"Nope," Mike said, leaning around me and lifting a hand to greet Mr. Zinbendal.

"How's your team doing?" Mr. Zinbendal asked when Mike plunked down on the futon.

Mike laughed. "I can't help thinking you already know the answer to that," he said. "They've had better seasons."

Mr. Zinbendal grinned.

They trash-talked each other's teams for a few minutes, which was fun to listen to when I wasn't checking on the food and setting the table.

Mom got there just minutes before everything was ready. She was in a good mood, which was a huge relief.

She chatted and laughed with the guys while I filled water glasses and scooped the rice into a bowl, put the salad on the table, and sat the pan with the chicken on a folded towel.

"Everything's ready," I announced, feeling proud. I'd been tempted to say that dinner was served, but decided at the last second it would sound dumb.

They all came to the table.

"This looks fantastic!" Mike said.

We passed stuff around and started to eat. Everything was really good.

It felt like it was going to be a great evening.

Twenty-eight

I'm not sure how long it took me to notice Mom's silence.

I'd been distracted by Mr. Zinbendal, who had a bit of rice on his chin. It was moving up and down, up and down when he chewed or talked and I kept waiting for it to fall, but it was on there like someone had glued it in place.

Mike was talking, but I'd missed the first part of what he was saying.

"It's true it's something of a lost art, but you never know. Interest in old hobbies can be revived suddenly, and in surprising ways."

"True, true," agreed Mr. Zinbendal, bobbing his head and the rice attached to it.

"Carving can be really relaxing too," Mike said.

That was when my attention shifted to my mother, probably nudged there by an instinctive warning system.

She was as still as a statue. Most of the food on her

plate was untouched, although she held her knife and fork upright at either side, as though she was posing for a photo. You'd have thought she was in a kind of trance, except for the fact that her eyes were blazing.

A jolt of cold sliced through me.

I tried frantically to think of some way to prevent whatever she was going to say or do. Because I knew. Whatever was coming was not going to be good.

It was hopeless. Panic had my brain on lockdown.

Mom's voice sounded distant at first. As though she was speaking from the edge of a tunnel. I doubt any of us would even have heard what she said, except for a pause in the conversation.

"I guess you all think I'm stupid."

Mr. Zinbendal's head turned toward her. He looked puzzled, but not yet alarmed. Mike, on the other hand, was instantly aware of what was happening. He's been through this before.

"I know exactly what you two are doing, so don't think you're fooling anyone."

"What are you saying, Rhea?" Mr. Zinbendal said. "Is something wrong?"

"Is something wrong?" Mom repeated, mocking him.

For a second or two there was silence. And then, like an explosion, the knife and fork Mom was holding were slammed down. Her hands smacked against the table as she stood.

"You two men think you can waltz in here and turn my own son against me?" she demanded. "Well, it's not happening. I've been watching and I know everything that's been going on. Everything!"

There was more. A torrent of words and movement. Accusations that made no sense — based on the splintered thoughts that had formed in my mother's tormented brain.

Poor Mr. Zinbendal tried to speak twice, which only angered her further. After the second time he shrunk back in his seat with his eyes focused downward.

Mike stood up without a word and stepped to Mr. Zinbendal's side. He reached a hand down and the old man took it and stood. They were on their feet just in time to obey my mother's harsh order for them to "Get out!"

I followed, just behind Mom, wanting to tell them how sorry I was about what was happening, but knowing if I did, I would only make matters worse. More than anything I wanted Mr. Zinbendal to know the person who'd just thrown him out was *not* the Rhea Hayes he'd been getting to know over the past couple of months.

Mike, of course, understood. He knew it wasn't Mom, but the torment of her illness taking control of her. Poor Mr. Zinbendal was another story, and I couldn't stand to think about what he must be feeling.

"And don't come back!" Mom snapped at their receding backs. "I see either one of you anywhere near my son again and I will call the police so fast your heads will spin."

The door closed behind them.

For the next few minutes I could barely hear my mother's labored breathing over the rushing, thundering sound of my own heartbeat. I didn't look at her and I didn't speak. Finally, I forced my legs back to the kitchen and cleared the table, saving as much of the food as I could salvage, because I knew what was ahead.

Mom stood in the doorway for a while, but I ignored her. Anything I said would only lead to a fight — especially the things I felt like saying then. It was my turn to do the dishes, but I left them stacked in the sink, got Sitta, and spent the rest of the evening in my room with the door shut.

Mom left me alone, which was a bit surprising. Maybe she could feel how totally furious I was with her.

That hadn't changed by bedtime. As I lay there I thought about the night Mom had been taken to the hospital. And I admitted something to myself that I hadn't thought about since then — the third reason I hadn't tried to get into the room when the ambulance workers were trying to revive my mother.

This is hard to say, but I'd had a brief, terrible thought that I didn't care if they saved her. In that split second of time, it didn't matter to me if my own mother was revived.

That might make me the worst son on the planet. It probably does.

The thought was gone as fast as it came, because I *do* love my mom. I just get so tired of living every day waiting for her to do the next thing that will tear our lives apart — again. I shouldn't have to be watching, tracking her moods, weighing and measuring everything she says and does. Sneaking around, counting pills.

The pills! I'd planned to wait until a week was up before counting them again, but it was obvious she wasn't taking her meds. The only thing left to find out was how badly she'd gone off track.

As quietly as I could, I got up and tiptoed to the hallway. I stood outside her room for what felt like an hour, listening hard. Finally, I nudged the door open and peeked in.

Mom was curled up with a blanket clutched around

her shoulders. She looked so peaceful and innocent in sleep. I felt a flash of regret for my earlier anger, even as I crept into the room and over to the closet. The bottles were on the shelf and I lifted them with as much caution as I could so as not to make a sound.

Ten minutes later I returned them to the spot where they'd been and went back to bed.

There was the exact same number of pills in each bottle as there had been when I'd checked them five days earlier.

Mom wasn't playing around with her dosage. She was off her meds completely.

Twenty-nine

I tried not to think about what it would mean if Mom hadn't left for work by the time I got up the next morning, but she was gone when I made my way to the kitchen.

So, she still had a job.

I filled the sink with hot soapy water and let the dishes soak while I had breakfast. It wasn't until I turned to open the cupboard that I noticed, sitting on the countertop, the cellophane package of cupcakes Mr. Zinbendal had brought for dessert the night before.

The sight of them was like a punch in the gut. I couldn't help picturing him, happily having dinner here one minute, and then the next, alone in his apartment, heartbroken and confused. There was no doubt in my mind becoming friends with us had meant a lot to him. It had meant a lot to me too.

For a moment I felt as if I couldn't breathe. It upset me so much I had to bend over the counter and clench my teeth to keep the roar in my throat from escaping.

How could I have been so stupid? It was as though I'd learned nothing … a big fat zero, from all the years of life with my mother.

The number one rule is always, always, always, not to get to know people. Not at school, not in the community, and especially not where we live. That is *never* going to lead to anything except embarrassment, shame, and disappointment.

As I slowly pulled myself together, I realized thoughts of breakfast were long gone. There was no way I could shove anything down at that moment, and I didn't feel like bothering with the dishes just then either. They could wait.

What I wanted to do, and did, was grab some paper and a pen and write a short letter to Mr. Zinbendal. If nothing else, he deserved an explanation.

Dear Mr. Zinbendal,

This is Corbin from across the hall. I just wanted to say I am so, SO sorry about last night. I should have told you this before, and maybe Mike already filled you in when my mom freaked out and kicked you guys out, but she has an illness called bipolar. It's not that uncommon so you probably know something about it. That's what makes her do strange or sometimes dangerous things, or act like she did yesterday. It happens when she goes off her meds, which I just found out she did again.

You're a really nice man and I liked it a lot when you came over here or we went over there. It kind of felt for a while almost like I had a grandfather.

I hope you don't mind if I thought of you that way. I still do, really, but my mom's illness makes it just about impossible to keep any kind of friendship going. Even if she comes around, I'll understand if you'd rather not risk putting your-self through that again. I know it had to be awful for you.

I'm sorry, too, about the cupcakes. No way I could even think about eating one after what happened, but I hope you can still enjoy them. I sure hope things work out with your daughter real soon.

Your friend, Corbin Hayes

I got ready for school then, and when I left the apart-ment I put the cupcakes and letter in a bag outside Mr. Zinbendal's door, knocked, and then ran down the hall so I'd be out of sight when he opened it. I knew I couldn't handle seeing his sad face. That was *not* the image I wanted to have in my brain all day.

I hate my mother.

I guess that will pass. It's not the first time I've been so mad at her that I felt that way, and it always fades eventually. (Because, of course, I don't really hate her, no matter how mad I get sometimes.) Besides, since I know what to expect from Mom, it's kind of my own fault. It's time I stopped thinking things are ever going to be different. Especially not better.

That evening was tense. Mom was in a dirty mood right from the minute she got home from work. (It's probably weird how thankful I am every day she hasn't quit her job. I doubt many kids my age even think about something like that.)

"Don't get on your high horse with me, Corbin," she warned. "I've got enough to deal with without your attitude."

"I didn't say anything," I answered.

I was getting our plates ready for supper; I'd mixed the leftover chicken and rice together with a bit of soy sauce and some corn.

"Exactly," she said. "You think you're getting away with ignoring me, think again."

"I'm not trying to ignore you," I said. I turned to face her and forced a smile. "I hope you're hungry because supper's ready."

She seemed to calm down, but while we ate she started talking about her job and that got her riled up again.

"They're all useless, I'm not kidding," she said angrily. "You wonder how they manage to get themselves dressed in the mornings. Maybe someone helps them."

"Probably," I agreed.

"I'm telling you, I'm the only one there who knows diddly-squat. It's like the rest of them are sharing a brain between them."

I did my best to laugh, which is not easy when you want to yell, "Just stop!" in someone's face.

"That bird is getting on my nerves," she said a few minutes later.

That seemed like a pretty random comment, since Sitta hadn't come into the kitchen once while we were eating. He seems to know when to stay away from Mom.

"Really?" I said, hoping I sounded surprised. "Because I can tell he likes you a lot."

This seemed to interest her. She wanted details, which I supplied as fast as I could make them up.

"He looks at you like this," I said, giving my head a jaunty shake, "which is bird body language for expressing affection. And I notice him nodding a lot when you're around. That shows approval."

"Huh!" Mom said. She seemed pleased.

For some reason, the smug look on her face made me angrier than anything she'd done earlier. I stared at her as she basked in the crazy notion that Sitta adored her. It was pathetic and self-centered and I couldn't take it for one more second.

"It never crosses your mind to put anyone else first, does it?" I said. It was surprising, how quiet my voice was when blood was roaring in my ears.

"What?" Mom looked startled as she lifted her face to meet my eyes. I don't know what she saw there, but it seemed to stop her in her tracks.

"You heard me. That scene last night? There was no need for that. None. We had guests, people I happen to like, but we couldn't have a nice, friendly meal, could we?"

Mom's mouth started to open.

"Don't!" I said. My voice was rising, but still reasonably calm. Even so, I knew she heard the current in it, the controlled fury.

"You never stop for one second to think about how

your choices affect me, do you?" I asked, not wanting or waiting for her to answer. "All you care about is how *you* feel. So you mess with your meds *every time*, and I have to live with the chaos that comes from that. Also every time."

Mom's eyes had filled with tears by then and, even though her hand was covering her mouth, I could tell her lips were trembling.

"Corbin, I swear —" she said.

I waited for her to finish. There wouldn't be anything new, anything believable in whatever denials or promises or excuses she might offer, but it didn't matter. Whatever she'd intended to say never made it into words. Her face crumpled as tears spilled over and ran down her cheeks.

There was more — a lot more — I could have said. More I wanted to say. But I was afraid if I really let loose I'd never get stopped, and if I did that I'd bury the point I'd made. So I ignored the tears, turned, and walked out of the room.

I had a chat with Sitta about the situation later.

"Tomorrow she'll act like none of this ever happened," I told him.

Sitta didn't answer, but he leaned forward and sideways so I knew he was listening. I went on.

"Things are sliding downhill, buddy. Any chance you've got another magic spell in you?"

Nothing.

"Come on, Sitta. Spell! Spell!" I chanted.

And then he said it.

"Spell! Spell!"

Thirty

Of course, I knew a bird repeating a word wasn't going to do anything. So I wasn't expecting anything to happen. Not seriously, anyway.

Which made it strange how disappointed I felt when nothing *did* happen. No unexpected shift in circumstances. No miraculous change in Mom. No sign that she'd decided to start taking her meds again.

I wondered, over the next few days, if maybe I was coming unhinged. How could I feel let down because my life didn't improve after a *parakeet* recited a random word?

But eventually I decided I probably wasn't teetering on the edge of sanity. I was desperate. Sick of the way things were and ready to grab onto any sliver of hope, no matter how small or silly.

Unfortunately, hope was in short supply. Since I've been on this ride forever, I knew what was ahead. The roller coaster of life with Mom was going to keep right on rising up, plunging down, and whipping around sharp corners. All I can ever do is hang on and wait for a chance to catch my breath.

I did what I always do when Mom starts to tilt and slide. I convinced myself I was ready. Except, this time I had more reason to think that than I usually do.

I was still working at the store a few hours a week, so produce for Sitta was taken care of, plus I'd started stockpiling the ten dollars worth of groceries I also earned there every week. I'd been stashing canned and dry foods in my closet, shoving them out of sight on the shelf and in the corners.

Besides that, I'd saved almost all of the babysitting money I'd made since back when Mom went into the hospital and Mike came to stay here. It wasn't a fortune, but I figured, with the food I had tucked away, I could stretch it for quite a while. With any luck it would be long enough to get us through the worst of things this time around.

None of that was going to keep us from getting kicked out of our apartment if Mom messed up on the rent, though. It didn't help knowing the chance she would do that was much greater than the chance she wouldn't.

I decided I'd try to talk with her about that as soon as I caught her in a calm, even pleasant frame of mind, which happened a few days later. The reason for her good mood was a bit of a shock.

She arrived home from work all smiles, as happy as I can remember seeing her in a long time. I watched curiously as she slung her purse on the futon and did a little dance around the living room. When she noticed me at the edge of the room she held a hand out.

"Care to dance with the new assistant manager of *So Fresh Cleaners*?" she asked with a joyous laugh.

"Seriously?"

"Yes, seriously!" She twirled and giggled. "Someone *finally* realized how much I have to offer."

"Well, that's great, Mom!" I smiled and tried to feel happy for her in spite of my instant apprehension.

Obviously Mom had convinced the store's owner she had some ideas that would be good for business. I doubted it would take long for that to fall apart.

Even so, when she grabbed my hand and drew me into the dance she was doing, I did my best to go along. I can usually let go of misgivings and just enjoy the happy moments. Not this time. The weight of dread was too heavy to throw off.

"I know *this* isn't a huge deal in itself," Mom said later over an oven pizza. "But it's a start — right? I've been waiting my whole life for someone to give me a chance to prove I can do things."

"I'm really glad for you, Mom," I said. "You definitely deserve this."

She reached over, squeezed my hand, and said, "Thanks, honey. And you know what — we can get a car soon because I'll be making more money."

"A car would be great," I said carefully. "And the best thing is, we *definitely* won't have to worry about moving."

"True," Mom said. "I remember you said something about how you like this place."

"I *really* do," I said. "That's why I want to stay here until I finish school."

"Right —" Mom pushed her plate away, although she'd eaten less than a third of her slice. She glanced around distractedly, and then stood up.

"You didn't eat much," I said.

"I've got things to do to get ready for my new responsibilities," Mom said. "I'll heat this up later if I'm hungry."

"Okay," I said, disappointed at how quickly she'd moved past my words. I'd hoped to reinforce the promise she'd made about staying here, to get her to feel a genuine commitment to doing that. Just in case it made any difference.

"Things are finally looking up for us, Corbin," Mom said. "Life hasn't exactly gone our way a lot of the time, but that's all going to change. Because once I prove what I can do at this place, I'll be in the ideal position to approach some bigger corporations with my ideas. There will be offers, of course, but I won't hire on with just one company."

Mom snapped her fingers. Her eyes shone with excitement.

"What I'm going to do is become a consultant, lending my expertise to Fortune 500 companies, sharing my methods with them, for a price of course."

Mom let out a small squeal just before she leaned down and whispered near my ear, "Son, we are going to be *rich*!"

I watched her dance down the hall to her room. Then I pushed my own plate away, appetite completely gone.

It was strange, even though things weren't anywhere near as bad as they've been other times, how it felt like that was the lowest moment of my life.

Thirty-one

Two weeks later Mom was unemployed and spending most of her time in bed or on the futon.

I could have predicted that. First there'd been the high, with all the manic thoughts and behaviors. It was a lot like watching a video in fast-forward, the way she launched into this whirl of activity, drawing up bizarre marketing plans, assembling training ideas and rules for the *So Fresh Cleaners* staff.

I was enlisted, as usual, as her test audience. She paced and raved, practicing presentations for meetings she planned to hold.

"Is that great or what!" she'd exult at the end.

"It sure is," I'd say. Meaning, of course, it was 100% "or what," though I was never foolish enough to say anything like that to her. She drew her own, happy conclusions.

I don't know how much of the babble and nonsense she tried to put in place at her dry cleaner's job. I only know her career as the assistant manager lasted one week and two days. When they finally figured out the golden girl's business plan was actually nothing but thinly disguised gibberish, they let her go. I honestly don't know what took them that long. They didn't even offer to put her back to her old job working the counter. Not that you could blame them.

I don't know if the end of her job had an effect on Mom or not, but the plunge that always follows her manic periods came almost at the same time as she was fired. She withdrew, barely spoke, and spent hours and hours lying around with a blanket over her. She watched television whenever she was in the living room — if you can call it "watching." She stared toward the TV, and it was turned on, but there was no reaction to anything that flickered across the screen.

At first I left her completely undisturbed, but after a few days I took a chance and changed the channel to something I wanted to see. A bit later she got up and wandered off to her room. After that, I put on whatever shows I liked. Sometimes she left, sometimes she stayed, but she never said a word about it.

It was the same old story in many ways. But not in *every* way.

In the past, worry was my normal response to Mom's quiet, depressed days. Worry about her and worry about people finding out what was going on — partly to protect Mom, but also out of my own shame and embarrassment. Because I didn't want to be the kid with a mother who does strange things. I was sure I'd be labeled some kind of freak by association.

This time, that changed.

It started at school, when my teacher asked to speak to me after class. He came around the front of his desk and half sat on it, looking casual and approachable.

"I've noticed you seem to be having trouble focusing in class the past week or so," he said.

"Sorry," I told him.

"No, no — I'm not lecturing you," he said. "I was simply concerned."

"Okay," I said. My eyes shifted to the floor and then to the doorway.

Mr. Cameron didn't take the hint.

"I'm in a better position to help if I know what difficulties a student might happen to be facing," he said.

"Okay," I said.

"These aren't just words, Corbin," he said.

That's all they were to me, but I didn't say so. I didn't say anything.

"Okay, I can see you don't feel like talking today," he said, "but the door is open if you ever do."

"Okay," I said. "Thanks."

There was a silent pause. Maybe he thought I'd suddenly start blabbing. As if.

"So, can I go?" I said when it started to get uncomfortable.

"Yes, of course."

Mr. Cameron stood up and walked me to the door, which told me he was probably going to try one more pitch before I got away. I wasn't wrong.

"Sometimes life is so confusing a person doesn't know who to trust. But those people are out there. You just need to figure out who they are."

I didn't answer. But as I walked home I kept hearing those words. At one point I stopped and stood still, and played back the whole conversation, right from the moment he came around his desk. The first thought that had crossed my mind was that he was positioning himself to look casual and approachable. As if it was part of a plan to *trick* me.

Why had I thought that?

I had *no reason* to think that. From what I've seen of

him, Mr. Cameron is a pretty stand-up guy: fair, patient, and decent to his class. So, why had my immediate, instinctive reaction been to distrust him?

I was almost home when I got it. No, that's not true. I think I already knew — maybe I'd always known, but had never been able to admit it before.

I'd been *trained* not to trust anyone. Trained by my mother's frequent struggles with paranoia, by my own embarrassment, and by the idea that the best strategy was always to keep our business hidden.

And that had made me see everyone on the "outside" as a kind of enemy.

"I'm trapped," I heard myself say. "I trapped myself!"

What a hopeless situation. For a couple of minutes I felt as if I couldn't get enough air into my lungs. My mother wasn't the only one to blame for the way things were — I was in there right alongside her, shoving people away, doing everything possible to keep our problems secret from the world. A partner in her illness.

Mr. Cameron's words circled back through my head and suddenly, like oxygen rushing back into my body, I realized something.

I had *already* trusted someone with the truth. Two people in fact. Izelle and Mr. Zinbendal.

I'd told Izelle enough about Mom's illness so that she

could understand how it affected things with Sitta.

And I'd told Mr. Zinbendal in the note I'd written to him — I hadn't even hesitated, because I'd wanted him to understand, and maybe feel less sad about what had happened.

I'd told two people and *nothing terrible had happened.* No agency had come along to take me to live with strangers. No snickers or whispers had followed me through the hallways at school. The sky hadn't fallen in.

Nothing bad — but also nothing good. I was in pretty much the same boat I'd been in when no one knew a thing. Still, it felt as though there'd been a change of some sort. I just couldn't figure out what it was.

Thirty-two

An illusion, I decided. That's what the change I'd imagined had been. Things were exactly as they'd always been.

All it took for me to reach that conclusion was to walk into the apartment and see my mother, draped across the futon, reaching listlessly into a box of oatmeal cookies. She glanced in my direction.

"There's my handsome son," she said.

"Hi Mom. How was your day?"

"So-so. I've been watching some home improvement shows," she said, taking a small bite of cookie and chewing slowly. "It's got me thinking."

"Oh, yeah? I'm going to get Sitta — you can tell both of us about it."

And she did, of course. I nodded and responded automatically while my mother, who knows nothing whatsoever on the subject, described how she was going to become a freelance home decorator. And make a fortune.

Being rich is always part of Mom's fantasies. Strangely, it's never part of mine, even though we've been down to practically nothing more than once. There are quite a few things ahead of wealth on my wish list.

My thoughts had drifted as Mom continued talking when, suddenly, she jerked upright, slapped her leg, and said, "Things *always* work out, even when it looks like they're not going to."

I'd have said the opposite. Just not out loud.

"Remember the gorgeous outfits I bought for my new position at the dry cleaner's?" she asked excitedly.

"I remember," I said, feeling my jaw tighten. It would have been hard to forget.

After two days as assistant manager, Mom had decided she needed to dress for success. Not so much for the dry cleaner's position, but because of the bigger and better things she just knew were right around the corner. The final result was a heap of clothes on the floor in her room, gaily tossed there after she'd strutted around, showing off each outfit.

Even if they hadn't gotten rumpled, there was no way I could have taken a bunch of women's clothes anywhere for a refund — supposing I'd been able to find the bags and receipts and figure out what was what.

"It's like I knew!" she said now, her eyes lit up and shining. "A premonition or something. Because nobody's going to hire a decorator who's not dressed for the part!"

Kind of like nobody's going to hire a decorator who's got zero training or experience, I thought, but didn't say.

I pulled myself to my feet and told Mom I was going to make supper. She followed me into the kitchen and sat at the table, talking about her new plan while I put fries and fish sticks on a cookie sheet and stuck it in the oven.

This was new. Not the upswing in Mom's energy and emotion, but the pattern. She'd already been up, and she'd slid down. The usual thing after that is she levels out enough to see the doctor and get back on her meds. But up, down, and now back up? I didn't know what to expect next. That was scary, because I'd always been able to count on, *plan* on even, the way one stage followed another.

As I put plates on the table I realized Mom had gone quiet. So, I told her it all sounded great, and she smiled this brilliant, bright smile and resumed talking. As scrambled as the world gets when she's up, that's when she feels genuinely happy and energized. Considering how she suffers at other times, it's impossible not to be glad she at least has that.

It was also impossible to ignore the fact that we were probably heading toward eviction. Except this time, I made up my mind to try to find out when it might be coming.

I hadn't talked to Mike since the night Mom threw him and Mr. Zinbendal out in the middle of dinner. In spite of her threat when he left, I thought he'd probably talk to me, so I took a chance and called him.

He didn't seem to mind. In fact, he sounded glad to hear from me, even when I told him why I was calling.

"Can you find out if Mom has enough money in the bank for the rent?"

"I don't know, Corbin," he said slowly. "Your mom only meant for me to access her account in emergencies."

"This *is* kind of an emergency," I said. "I really don't want to have to leave here, and I've been saving my babysitting money, so if we're just a bit short on the rent I might be able to make up what's missing. But if there's enough, I'll use my money for other things."

Mike hesitated, but then he told me to hang on. I heard tapping at a keyboard and a muttered sound that wasn't encouraging, and then he came back.

"There's just under fifty bucks in there," he said.

"Did she already get this month's child support? And that benefit thing?"

"Yes. Sorry. They've been spent."

So. Eviction is almost certainly coming up. We might squeak by if Mom levels out, gets another job, and scrapes up what she owes really quick, but I knew that wasn't likely. I wondered if there was any chance I could persuade her to look for another place in the same general area if we got kicked out of this building. So I could keep my jobs. So I could stay in the same school. So I could still have the few friends I'd made.

Izelle and, in a way, Taylor. And Mr. Zinbendal. If we lived nearby it would be easy for me to visit without Mom knowing, if it was okay with him.

Since Izelle knew about Mom, I decided to alert her to what was coming. Not just because she deserved to know, but because she was someone safe to talk to.

I waited a few days, until her regular visit with Sitta. Since Mom was in the apartment there was no chance to say anything until the visit was over and Izelle was ready to leave.

"I'll walk you downstairs," I said.

She glanced at me a couple of times before we got to the lobby. It looked like she was about to ask what was up but, for a chatty person, she managed to wait until I spoke.

I waited until we were outside, where I could be sure no one else would overhear.

"You must have noticed my mom hasn't been doing so great lately," I said, trying to ease into it.

"I did," she said. "Is it very —?"

"Bad? Yeah. She lost her job earlier in the month and she's been, well, really struggling."

Saying more than that would have felt like a betrayal, so I moved on.

"Chances are pretty good we'll be getting kicked out of our apartment soon."

"Oh no!" Izelle's eyes flashed with alarm. And concern. "Do you have any idea where you'll go if that happens?"

"That's what I wanted to tell you," I said. I couldn't look her in the eye. "Usually when we move, Mom wants to go to another part of the city. That way she knows she won't run into anyone who knows what happened."

"So I might not get to see Sitta — hardly ever," she said slowly. Then her head snapped up. "Oh! Corbin, I'm so sorry — thinking about myself when you've got all this to deal with!"

"Actually, I've been thinking, it would be better for everyone if you found another home for Sitta. Somewhere stable, and where you can keep seeing him. That's only fair."

Izelle stared at me. "Do you *want* to give him back?" she asked.

Not even a little bit.

"Kind of," I said. "I mean, he's a great bird and everything, but it's just one more thing for me to worry about and take care of when things get rough."

"Corbin, are you sure?" she asked. Her eyes were so sad. I couldn't look at her.

"I'm sure," I said. "I've got enough to handle without a pet. Even one like Sitta."

"How soon do you want him gone?"

Never. Never, *never*, never.

"The sooner the better," I told her.

Thirty-three

I did my best to explain the situation to Sitta.

"You'll be better off," I told him. "I mean, you've seen what it's like here. Some days are great, but the bad ones can get pretty dismal. That's not fair to you, buddy."

Sitta helped himself to a piece of baby spinach and ate it with no sign of concern.

"That's right," I said, "you'll be cool with it. You know how to take things in stride. And don't worry, Izelle will still get to visit you. So it's not like you'll be completely among strangers."

Unlike me.

But so what? Being surrounded by strangers was my normal. Why I'd let myself make the mistakes I'd made here on Westlester was beyond me. I knew better than to make friends, get to know neighbors, let people in. The bottom line was, it had always been me and Mom against the world. Because family is the thing that matters the most, and she was all I had.

I wouldn't forget that the next time. Classmates and pets and games of cribbage with a lonely old guy across the hall — who needed them? All that does is leave a person feeling like he's been kicked in the gut when it's time to walk away.

I wonder how long it takes for a toddler to forget someone completely. Molly will probably have no recollection of me in no time. It will be like "Cobin" never existed in her world.

Man, I hope that kid has a great life.

"Call, call," Sitta said. He'd probably noticed my focus had drifted. He can be a bit of an attention hog at times, that bird.

"I told you before, there's no one to call," I reminded him.

"Spell?" he said. It sounded like a question.

A laugh got out past the lump in my throat.

"Yeah, a spell is exactly what we need," I said. "Except, we both know there's no real magic in the world. If there was, I have no doubt whatsoever you'd be in charge of it."

Sitta gave me a nod and took to the air. It's amazing,

how birds lift off, and I watched him make a couple of loops around the room before heading down the hall to see if there was anything new in the rest of the apartment.

It had felt like a real home for a while. Another mistake I wouldn't let myself repeat.

That made me wonder how quick this landlord would be about evicting us. Some were lightning fast, others cut you a bit of slack. Either way, it was close enough to the end that I'd be able to finish the school year at Middling, which was one small thing to be thankful about.

Izelle let me know a couple of days later that she had arrangements coming together for Sitta.

"Can you keep him for a bit longer, though?" she asked. "So there's time to get everything organized?"

I shrugged. "I guess," I said, like it didn't much matter one way or the other. But it annoyed me a bit. What was the big delay? If someone wanted Sitta, they should be excited to get him as soon as possible. I sure hoped Izelle hadn't found him a home that wasn't going to appreciate him.

I didn't ask anything about it, though. To be honest, I've kind of pulled back from being so chummy with

Izelle. Not because she's done anything wrong, but seriously, what's the point?

It's Mom I need to be concentrating on anyway. She didn't stay "up" very long this time and I'm hoping I'm right about the first drop being brought on by the loss of her last job. It's going to be hard to handle things if the ups and downs start being unpredictable. You can prepare yourself a lot better if you know what's coming next.

Her interior decorating idea folded and faded into nothing in about three days. After that she went back to lying around, staring at the TV, sleeping, and picking at her food. I got a package of brownie mix and made that for her. Brownies are one thing she'll almost always eat.

I mentioned Mike to her once, to see where she was at, but she didn't take the bait.

So for now, everything is a waiting game.

Waiting for Mom to get past the slump and back on track.

Waiting for Izelle to take Sitta to his new home.

Waiting for a notice on the door that says we're out of here.

The only thing I've finally learned to stop waiting for is change.

Thirty-four

We're now over a week into June and so far no eviction notice has been posted. I almost wish it would hurry up and come. I just want to get this over with.

It's Monday, so Izelle came over after school. I told her to go ahead and get Sitta while I checked on Mom. She was in bed when I got home and I wanted to make sure everything was okay. It was.

Not that there's much danger. She's not nearly as low as she gets sometimes — it's more like she's really, really tired. More importantly, I swiped her meds and hid them. Non-prescription stuff too. All out of reach for now.

Izelle came into the living room with Sitta perched on her thumb after she'd fed him.

"When's he moving to his new home?" I asked.

"Things should be settled this week," she said. She kissed his beak and he leaned in as if he was looking into her eyes.

I smiled in spite of myself.

"I'm glad you're going to be able to keep seeing him," I said.

Izelle turned to face me, something she'd avoided doing lately. I know she feels the difference between us, the stiffness and pulling away. I like to think she understands, and isn't hurt or angry about it.

"Me too," she said lightly. Then her face changed and she took a deep breath.

"You know, it's because of Sitta that we got to be friends," she said.

I made no comment.

"We *are* friends, right?" she pressed.

"Sure," I said. Dismissively.

"It's important you know that," she said. "That I'm your friend, I mean."

"Did you give Sitta fresh water?" I asked.

She got it. Subject closed. It was a strange conversation anyway, even for Izelle. My guess was that she was feeling bad about Sitta's upcoming move. Maybe she felt guilty about it, although there was no reason for her to since it had been my idea.

The rest of the visit went okay. No more awkward talk about friendship at least. When she left I told Sitta not to mind her.

"She's an emotional type," I said, while he stood on one of my shoes. "But she seriously *cares*, so you've gotta overlook it when she gets all heartfelt and stuff."

Sitta gave me a wise look. He understands a lot, that bird, but before he could say anything, Taylor's familiar knock came at the door.

To prove how smart he is, Sitta flew straight to our room. He seems to know when someone knocks he's going to be tucked away somewhere secure.

"Hey," Taylor said when I opened the door. "Can you come down to my place?"

"I have to make supper," I said. "Can you bring Molly here?"

"It's not to watch Molly," she said. "Come on, it will just take a few minutes."

I hesitated, decided not to bother disturbing Mom if it was going to be that quick, and followed Taylor.

"What's up?" I asked.

"It'll be easier to explain when we get there," she said.

And then we were there and inside. Molly raced to me with her usual excitement, but my brain was busy taking in what else was happening.

"Don't be mad," came a timid voice.

The speaker was Izelle, who'd left my place only minutes before. She was in the corner of the living room, next to Taylor's mom, Sandra. Mr. Zinbendal was across from them and walking toward me was Mike. Taylor had planted herself behind me, like a guard or something.

"What's going on?" I demanded. I might have said something angrier, but Molly was there. And it was the first time I'd seen Mr. Zinbendal since the night Mom flipped out. The look on his face got to me.

"We just have a few things we want to say," Mike said. It seemed he'd been given the role of spokesperson in this ambush. "But before that, we need to make sure there's no one here who shouldn't be."

I imagine the confusion showed on my face.

"So, Corbin, is there anyone here who you wouldn't help, if they needed it?"

"What?"

He repeated the question. I looked around the room.

"Of course not," I said.

"You'd help *all* of us?" Mike confirmed. "For sure?"

"Yes, but —"

"What if I needed help?" Mr. Zinbendal said. "What if I fell and hurt myself, but I told you to leave me alone?"

"I'd still —" I stopped. "You tricked me," I said.

Mr. Zinbendal smiled. "No," he said. "Your heart spoke. Now, let our hearts speak to you."

Izelle, who was clearly behind getting everyone together, told me she was sorry for betraying a confidence, but she'd done it out of friendship and caring.

"Just like if I fell and you needed to get someone to help me," Mr. Zinbendal pointed out.

Taylor told me she was disappointed in me and a bit mad, but she was getting over it and I should have trusted her because it would have taken pressure off if there were times I couldn't babysit and whatnot. It wasn't the most organized speech ever, but she got her point across.

Sandra told me she was going to make an effort to get to know Mom, to be a friend and sounding board and do what she could to help make things run a bit steadier.

"But we won't be here," I pointed out.

Then Mike told me he'd gotten a message through to my father, that the rent was paid and my dad was coming to see me and get some things worked out as soon as he could get away.

That was when Izelle admitted she hadn't looked for another home for Sitta at all, so he wasn't really going anywhere.

And Mr. Zinbendal said, as the oldest one there, he

was also the wisest. Everyone smiled at that. Also, he told me the people in that room were my friends — that, in fact, they were more than my friends, they were my family.

Their hearts sure had a lot to say.

Thirty-five

As promised, my father showed up ten days later.

Mom was on the futon. She was still a bit down, but she'd restarted her meds and I could see she was starting to come out of the slump. She'd made up with Mike and apologized to Mr. Zinbendal, which were huge signs she was on her way to leveling out.

"That's your father," she said as soon as the knock came. I wondered how she knew.

Sitta was down the hall so I went straight to open the door. Mom was right.

"Corbin," Dad said.

"Hi," I said. Not exactly a warm greeting from either side.

"I've got a rental car outside — can we go for a drive?" he said.

A few minutes later, after he'd spoken briefly with Mom, he and I were pulling into the street and heading out of the city. My father never likes to be in what he calls the concrete jungle.

"You didn't get my email?" he said as he pointed the car north. "I was off the grid for a while, but I answered right away once I finally got yours."

So he *had* answered me. Eventually. After sending my angry message, I'd stopped checking for a reply when there'd been none in the first few weeks. I told him that.

"We clearly need to talk about some things," he said.

"Talk isn't going to fix anything," I said. The anger I'd felt back when I'd sent that email was building in me again, just from remembering the things I'd written — all completely justified.

"I know you understand that I have to work, son," he said.

I shrugged.

"And you were right. I haven't been around. I haven't been much of a father. I don't blame you for feeling I abandoned you in a bad situation."

"Because you did," I said evenly.

"Look, Corbin, what can I say? I'm sorry. The fact is, not everyone is cut out to be a parent. But I do care about you. I know that's hard for you to see, but it's true. You're my son and I love you."

"Sorry if that doesn't give me warm fuzzies," I said. "But whatever you claim to feel, I still have a mother who's sick a lot of the time and a father who's never around."

He was silent for a good ten minutes, maybe longer. I thought of lots of things I wanted to say during that time, but I was determined to outlast him in saying nothing.

Eventually he pulled onto a side road that wandered through the countryside, which seemed to relax him, and he spoke again.

"I don't know what to tell you," he said. "This doesn't seem to be a situation that can change unless I leave my job, which I, frankly, am not prepared to do. My work is important to me and it's at a stage where I just can't leave it."

"Glad something's important to you," I said. "Do you know how many times I've had to move, and change schools, and start over? I basically grew up without friends because we move so much. My grades are all over the place. But at least your work is important."

The next silence was different. I could see he was thinking hard, but there didn't seem to be much point to it. Unless he was going to be around, what could he do to make things better?

That's what I thought, anyway.

It turned out there were things he could do. And he seemed pretty embarrassed he'd never figured any of that out before. Which was fine — I'd lived with plenty of embarrassment over the years, it was someone else's turn.

He didn't quit his job. He didn't make himself a whole lot more available either, although he promised to do better than he had until now. But what he did do took a lot of pressure off me.

He set things up so that from then on part of his support payment went directly to cover the rent. We'd never have to be evicted for non-payment again.

He got me a cell phone and a tablet and set up a wifi account for them. That was huge for me — home access to the internet, which most folks take for granted, was something I'd never had before. Or a phone to reach out with if I needed help, and to stay connected to people in my life.

He also set up a joint bank account for me and him. He put four hundred dollars in it, as a backup for essentials like food, and he promised to keep an eye on it and replenish it if he saw I'd had to use it.

I thanked him for all of that, and I meant it. Even though he's not involved the way I think a father should be, he's doing something to make my path easier.

It doesn't make him a hero, but then there are other heroes in this story. Those are the people who cared, and stepped up to help a kid who was lost in his struggles.

The people whose hearts spoke to me.

Habits die hard. I've been finding that out day by day and you know what? The hard part is mostly remembering.

Remembering not to keep making the same mistakes that isolated me for so long. Remembering that it's okay to trust.

Remembering that there can be ties every bit as strong as blood ties.

Acknowledgements

The idea for *Birdspell* sprang from a brainstorming chat with the very gifted Ann Featherstone. I've had the pleasure of working with Ann on only one of my stories (*Tumbleweed Skies*) but some of the things I learned from her have influenced my writing ever since. Ann, you are a rare treasure.

Once written, *Birdspell* found a home with DCB Young Readers and the stellar group of folks there! Barry Jowett worked his editorial magic, directing my attention to flaws without actually calling them such (thanks) and offering guidance that strengthened the story considerably. Sarah Jensen did a lovely job on the copyedit and Andrea Waters added her expert touch without once complaining about the many, many commas she had to add. (I have tried, but never with any success, to develop a greater fondness for commas.) Behind the scenes, doing mysterious and wonderful things, were Sarah Cooper and Chantelle Cho. Thanks to all of you, and also to David Jardine for the fantastic cover art!

Taking a story from concept to completion requires time and focus. For the assistance that made this project possible, I gratefully acknowledge the support of the New Brunswick Arts Board.

VALERIE SHERRARD was born in 1957 in Moose Jaw, Saskatchewan, and grew up in various parts of Canada. Her father was in the Air Force so the family moved often, and was sent to live in Lahr, West Germany, in 1968. There, her sixth grade teacher, Alf Lower, encouraged her toward writing, although many years would pass before she began to pursue it seriously.

Valerie's debut YA novel was published in 2002. Since then, she has expanded her writing to include stories for children of all ages.

Valerie Sherrard's work has been recognized on national and international levels and has been translated into several languages. She has won or been shortlisted for numerous awards, including the Governor General's Award for Children's Literature, the Canadian Library Association Book of the Year for Children, the TD Canadian Children's Literature Award, the Geoffrey Bilson, the Ann Connor Brimer, and a wide range of readers' choice awards.

Valerie currently makes her home in New Brunswick with her husband, Brent, who is also an author.

We acknowledge the sacred land on which Cormorant Books operates. It has been a site of human activity for 15,000 years. This land is the territory of the Huron-Wendat and Petun First Nations, the Seneca, and most recently, the Mississaugas of the Credit River. The territory was the subject of the Dish With One Spoon Wampum Belt Covenant, an agreement between the Iroquois Confederacy and Confederacy of the Ojibway and allied nations to peaceably share and steward the resources around the Great Lakes. Today, the meeting place of Toronto is still home to many Indigenous people from across Turtle Island. We are grateful to have the opportunity to work in the community, on this territory.

We are also mindful of broken covenants and the need to strive to make right with all our relations.